S+AKE YOUR DES+INY

THE SUICIDE KING

Buffy the Vampire Slayer™

Available from POCKET BOOKS

STAKE YOUR DESTINY

THE SUICIDE KING

Robert Joseph Levy

An original novel based on the hit television series
created by Joss Whedon

POCKET
BOOKS

LONDON NEW YORK SYDNEY TORONTO

POCKET
BOOKS

An imprint of Simon & Schuster
Africa House, 64–78 Kingsway, London WC2B 6AH

www.simonsays.co.uk

™ & © 2005 Twentieth Century Fox Film Corporation. All Rights Reserved. All rights reserved, including the right of reproduction in whole or in part in any form.

POCKET BOOKS and related logo are trademarks of Simon & Schuster, Ltd

Printed and bound in Great Britain

First Edition   10 9 8 7 6 5 4 3 2 1

A CIP catalogue record for this book is available from the British Library

ISBN 1-4165-0242-4

Acknowledgments

The author would like to thank Joss Whedon, the cast and crew of *Buffy the Vampire Slayer,* and everyone at Mutant Enemy for allowing him to inhabit the breathtaking world they so lovingly created.

Special thanks to the Head, the Hand, and the Heart that guided this project from its inception: Tricia Boczkowski, Patrick Price, and Dan Sacher.

NOTE TO THE READER

S+AKE Y⊕UR DES+INY

Into every generation a chosen one is born who will stand alone against the vampires, the demons, and the forces of darkness. In this generation it's you, Buffy Summers of Sunnydale, California—high school student by day, Slayer of the undead by night. It's a tough gig, but somebody's gotta do it.

Now, this sacred birthright thing comes with a few rules: Always listen to your Watcher, never fall in love with a vampire, and, whatever you do, do not read this book in sequential order.

Okay, you can ignore those first two rules, but the last is nonnegotiable. Make sure to follow the messages at the bottom of the page—they'll let you make a choice regarding the story line, giving you a different page to turn to depending on what action you decide to take. As usual, the fate of the world is in your hands, so choose carefully. And isn't it about time you got to make your own decisions?

Break a leg—just make sure it's not your own.

Turn to page 1. . . .

Prologue

Diana Fitzgerald usually brushes her teeth every evening before going to sleep, but tonight is different. Instead she just turns up the faucet, hot, letting it run for a few minutes while she stares at herself in the bathroom mirror. She remembers when she used to think she was reasonably good-looking. Sure, she had her fleeting struggles with bad skin, and when it rained her hair went all frizzy, but she always found that the attractiveness pendulum would eventually swing back her way. Not anymore. No matter what her boyfriend, Gary, says, no matter what even the mirror shows her, she knows she is hideous, deformed, a freak of nature never meant to show its face. The steam from the hot water begins to cloud the mirror, and Diana watches with remote satisfaction as her face disappears in the reflection, dissolving away into a gray fog. She shuts off the tap and opens the bathroom door, heading up the narrow staircase to her bedroom on the top floor of her family's three-story colonial on Bernadine Drive.

Once inside her room she closes the door behind her and leans against it, taking in the space that used to feel like a sanctuary of sorts, a safe place squirreled away from the rest of the house and all the dangers of the outside world. Now this sense of security has become just another carefully disguised illusion, like school, her family, her relationship with Gary. These things are false, transparencies, the belief in them a kind of self-willed delusion she has erected in order to ward off the unfathomable void that lies just beneath the surface. Underneath, that's where the darkness lives. The darkness is all that's real anymore.

Time to give up.

She goes over to her desk, past the wall of shelves displaying her many awards, mostly for tennis and drama. She has a distant recollection of pride at winning such prizes, but no memory of what that sensation feels like, only that it must have once existed. And then Diana remembers she's won a competition to have a play she wrote performed at a festival of young playwrights. She remembers receiving a letter in the mail telling her she's won and will be flown to New York in a month. She had been flabbergasted, thrilled, and had immediately begun planning her trip—how she was going to spruce up her script, which sights she was going to see in New York, what she was going to wear. . . . And now she feels nothing inside, no excitement, no trepidation. . . . Did that letter, once so important to her, arrive only one short week ago?

Time to write the letter.

Sitting at her desk, she begins to write a letter of her own, to everyone she's ever known: Gary, her parents, her friends at school. It may be the most important work she's ever produced, yet she takes no time in writing it, only hurrying toward its completion, so that it will be done, once and for all. She signs her name, folds the paper, and tucks it into an envelope, which she marks "PLEASE READ." Her gaze moves up to the bulletin board hanging above her, its surface covered corner to corner with photographs: her parents and her with her two sisters, Polaroids of her friends, pictures of her and Gary that they took over the summer in a photo booth at the mall. She feels something then, as she stares at the faces of her loved ones, a faint fluttering in her chest, a sigh, a hint of regret perhaps.

Time to open the drawer.

The sensation is gone. She reaches down and slides open the top drawer of her desk, her hand moving around inside it, searching out the one thing she knows she must find. And there it is; she tightens her grip around its handle, the touch of it cool against the skin of her palm. She slides the drawer shut, stands, and walks over to her bed, placing the envelope on her pillow, the words "PLEASE READ" staring up at her in bold black print. She feels something pass over her, like an impossible noonday shadow stretching languidly beneath the warm glow of the sun. For a moment it's almost as if she forgets who she is, or what she's doing there, standing in the middle of her room, the heavy blanket of night pressing down just outside her windows. But then she sees the letter she left on her pillow and feels the weight of the silver letter opener in her hand, and she suddenly remembers, *Oh, yes, that's right.*

Diana Fitzgerald, seventeen years old and an honor student at Sunnydale High, raises the letter opener in her hand and plunges it into her skull.

SLAYER ACTION:
Turn to page 5.

You have something stuck in your head and you can't get it out. Not like a pickax or a piece of shrapnel, but rather something far more painful, far more insidious: a Barry Manilow song. It lodged itself there last night when you went patrolling with Angel; he was whistling a tune that started as a haunting Irish lullaby and ended as the chorus of "Mandy." You could forgive a lot of things that come out of that vampire-with-a-soul's mouth, but this isn't one of them.

Luckily you have an early-morning meeting that should take your mind off this affliction that's plagued you since you woke up: a before-school hookup with Giles and the rest of the Scoobies to discuss your plans for destroying a recently discovered vamp nest. You (and Mandy, unfortunately) head down the hall and through the swinging doors of the sparsely frequented Sunnydale High library, ready to talk shop, only to find the gang sitting silently at the long study table. On one side Xander stares mournfully up at the ceiling; across from him are Willow and Cordelia, both with distant, listless expressions on their faces. It's as quiet as a morgue.

"What's with the stone cold, guys? Who died?" They look up at you. More silence. "I should really stop asking that."

"One of your fellow students, actually." Rupert Giles, your Watcher, steps out from behind the circulation desk. "Apparently another suicide."

"Anyone we know?" you ask.

"Diana Fitzgerald," Willow says. "She takes trig with me."

"She's also a theater chick," Cordelia adds, "but

not the 'I wear black on the outside because black is how I feel on the inside' type. More like, 'I can't wait to see all my old friends from acting camp this summer!'" She conveys this impression with her best jazz hands aflutter.

"So why go all last-page Willy Loman, then?" you ask.

"Good question," Willow replies. "Especially because she was really psyched about this playwriting thingy she had coming up. She told me all about it before class a week ago. She was so excited. It just doesn't make any sense." The expression on Willow's face—a cross between sadness and confusion—puts knots in your stomach.

"Who needs a reason anymore?" Cordelia says, flipping her obsessively groomed mane of dark hair over one shoulder. "What is this, the third suicide this month? It's practically a fad. It's the latest thing to do."

"Ah, yes, how true," Xander muses. "Offing yourself: It's this year's trucker cap."

"Cordelia has a point," Giles says. "It certainly seems as if suicide has become quite prevalent here in recent weeks. A trend, indeed. Due to the burden of life on the Hellmouth, perhaps?" He checks his pocket watch. "It's time for the assembly."

"Time for the what now?" you ask.

"Didn't you hear? The principal called a special schoolwide assembly to address the recent suicides."

"Great," you say, rolling your eyes. "Snyder and compassion: together at last."

• • •

"Sit down before I make you sit down!" Principal Snyder stalks back and forth across the stage of the school auditorium, intermittently lunging toward the podium in order to bark something into the microphone. Standing onstage beside him is a tall, thin man dressed in khakis and a button-down shirt, forty years old maybe and balding. You and your friends take seats near the back, while Giles scuttles off, having spotted his girlfriend, Jenny Calendar, on the other side of the room.

"By now," Snyder begins, "you've probably all heard about what happened to your classmate Diana Fitzgerald, the third Sunnydale High student to take her own life in the past month. The school board has brought in a guest speaker to address this problem, as well as answer any questions you may have. You will each have individual appointments with him throughout the rest of the week, and these meetings are *mandatory,* people. You can find your appointment times on the bulletin board in the hall outside the auditorium directly following this assembly. Now, please show the proper respect—that includes you, mister—," Snyder says, eyes narrowing, to a boy in the front row, "for Doug Teal of the California Mental Health Association."

The guy in the khakis steps up to the podium and smiles sadly at the crowd. "Thank you, Principal Snyder. I know some of you are very upset, and I don't want to take up too much of your time. Everyone grieves in their own way, and that's okay. You may feel confused, or guilty, or even lucky. These are all normal emotions. And I look forward to discussing these feelings over the course of the coming days.

"But before we leave here today, I want to take a few moments to read to you the note Diana left before she took her own life." He reaches into his breast pocket and takes out a folded piece of paper. " 'Dear Everyone, I just want you to know that it's time for me to go now. I can't fight it anymore, and this is the only way I know how to stop it. Do not let it get to you, too.' "

You wait your turn to check the bulletin board. Your appointment with the crisis counselor is scheduled for 4:00 P.M. in the principal's office. "Yikes," you say to the others. "I'm supposed to be working on a project later for art class, and I haven't even started."

"No problemo," Willow says. "Why don't we swap. I'll take your appointment today, and you can have mine Thursday afternoon."

"Maybe I should just suck it up and go. Honestly, I'd rather get it over with, and if I skip patrolling tonight I should have enough time to get the project done."

"Or, you can blow it off and come see the new Gwyneth movie that just opened at the Sun," Cordelia suggests. "Due to all the heavy drama, of course."

"Oh, no!" Xander moans, hanging his head. "Please tell me it's not going to be chick-flick night. Why not just be up-front about it and say you don't want me around?"

"We don't want you around," Cordelia replies without the faintest trace of sarcasm.

"Why, Miss Chase, I do believe you're flirting with me."

"Not if you were the last loser on earth."

"Whoa, there, Cordy. I was just kidding." Xander retreats a few paces backward. "Besides, I can always tell when you're flirting by the intoxicating aroma of skunk pheromones in the air."

Willow rolls her eyes before stepping between Cordelia and Xander and moving to your side. "So, what's it going to be, Buffy?" Willow asks. "Do you want to keep your appointment or trade with me? Or," she says, a mischievous smile passing over her face, "maybe it's Scooby movie night? Huh? Is it? Huh? Huh?" Willow grabs your arm and starts bouncing up and down. She's clearly been dipping into the secret stash of candy corn she keeps at the bottom of her locker.

SLAYER CHOICE:

Do you decide to . . .

❚ swap your grief-counselor appointment with Willow's so you can work on your art project after school? *If yes, turn to page 10.*

❚ suck it up and keep your appointment? *If yes, turn to page 14.*

❚ blow off both and go catch a movie with the gang? *If yes, turn to page 56.*

Now that you and Willow have swapped appointments, you have all afternoon to get going on that art project that's due in two days. After your last class, you head over to the art studio, which is empty. You close the door behind you and go over to the stretch of shelves below the windows for your supplies, in this case a large pad of paper and a couple of pieces of charcoal. Sliding behind one of the long worktables, the surface stained by years of spattered paint and dried clay, you sit in front of the blank page and stare at it, thinking about the daunting task ahead. The assignment: Draw something that you have strong feelings about, but that is not a person or an animal. You exhale loudly. Your teacher, Mr. Blodgett, flippantly announced the assignment at the end of last class, and no one else seemed to be particularly thrown by it. But you are. Maybe if the bell hadn't already rung you would've asked him for an example, or at least an example of an example. So now you just continue to stare at the white emptiness of the paper.

Okay, strong feelings. What do I have strong feelings about? you think. *Well, I have strong feelings about Angel. Strong, slightly mushy, sometimes painful, but generally warm feelings. And I have strong feelings about my friends. And Giles. And Mom. I care about all of them. Strongly. But these are all people. Even Angel, as far as Mr. Blodgett is concerned.*

You begin to think about what you have negative strong feelings about: vampires, demons, creatures of the night. . . . You probably couldn't adequately explain why you feel strongly about these things in and of themselves. But then you realize what it is: These things bring fear. Specifically, fear of loss, fear of death, fear of losing those close to you.

So you begin to draw. It starts as a wide vertical line slashing across the page, spiraling down toward a point located on a dark and distant plane. Then, you create some rounded horizontal shapes negotiating the empty space around the thick line, conveying a sense of movement, of things rushing off, beyond control, away. Okay, you're getting close to what you're trying to show; the page has an abstract rendering of loss, but no immediacy, no sensation of fear. So how do you convey fear without depicting a person or an animal? And besides, there's still too much white space left; if there's any hard and fast rule in Mr. Blodgett's class, it's don't turn in any work with too much blank space.

Maybe you're getting hung up on the concept because you're really just worried about disappointing your mother. She was the art geek in high school—you've got a basement filled with old canvases to prove it—and if you get another C in art, she's going to give you that heartbreakingly sad "Oh, Buffy," usually accompanied by a tilt or soft shaking of the head. Anything to avoid that.

Just then you hear the sound of someone crying coming from the hallway outside the studio. You get up—secretly eager to have a distraction from your work—and poke your head out the door. At the end of the hall is the distressing sight of Willow Rosenberg, your best friend, standing at her locker bawling uncontrollably. You hurry to her.

"Will, what is it? Was it your meeting?" She nods slowly and lets out another barely stifled sob. "Pretty intense, huh?" You rub her back, trying to get her to let it all out. "Those must have been some heavy issues he had you discussing."

"It wasn't that," she manages to get out between the tears. "It was the grief counselor."

"What? What did he do to you? What did he say?" Your mind begins to race.

"He's dead." Willow reaches into her pocket and removes a tattered tissue, using it to dab at her nose. "I was waiting outside the principal's office, where the meetings are held, and it was taking so long since the last student came out that I thought, well, I'll just get up and knock on the door. So I did, and there was no answer, and I opened the door a crack and I saw . . . I saw . . ."

"What did you see?" you say after a few moments.

Willow looks at you, but with a faraway stare in her eyes. "He was hanging from the ceiling fan, Buffy. I think he killed himself."

"Oh my God."

"It just doesn't make any sense. I mean, he's a grief counselor. Why would he . . . He seemed fine at the school assembly, didn't he?"

"He sure did. There could be more to it. This being Demonville, USA, and all." You think for a moment, then say, "I better go check out his office. Are you going to be okay by yourself for a little while?"

"Sure, Buff," she says, still sniffling. "I'll be fine."

In spite of what she says, however, she sure doesn't *look* okay. Not at all. You probably only have a few minutes to check out the principal's office before the trusty Sunnydale police and coroner's offices get all *CSI* on the place. But Willow . . . She doesn't appear to be quite with it.

SLAYER CHOICE:

Do you decide to . . .

❘ take Willow at her word and go check out the principal's office, finding out what you can about the grief counselor's death? *If yes, turn to page 14.*

❘ walk Willow home and, if you have enough time, return to school for some reconnaissance? *If yes, turn to page 93.*

The door to the principal's office is open, just a crack. "Hello?" you say. When you get no response, you use the toe of your boot to slowly push the door open. The room is bathed in an eerie, diffuse afternoon light, and your eyes need a moment to adjust before focusing on the shocking image before you. Hanging from the ceiling fan, in startling full view, is the grief counselor who introduced himself to the school at the assembly just a few short hours ago. You walk slowly toward the center of the room, all the while staring up at him, mesmerized by the barely perceptible motion of his slightly swaying body. You see then that he is hanging by his necktie, tied in a coarse but obviously durable knot around the motor in the center of the fan. Your gaze travels down to the upended chair on the floor below him. Sure looks like suicide, but, this being Sunnydale, you're well aware of how deceiving appearances can be. Best to check for clues.

You walk over to the desk and see a stack of pamphlets, photocopies on colored paper. You pick up one of the pamphlets, and see "Depressed?" written across the front; another says "Anxious?" while a third says "Lonely?" You open up "Lonely?" and read some of the text inside.

> *You're not alone. Millions of people from all walks of life experience feelings of despondency, listlessness, and fear that they are unable to control. But you need not suffer in silence. Talk to your teachers, friends, and family about your problems, and seek out someone in the helping professions (counselor,*

psychologist, social worker) who can offer you com-
fort and advice that will ease your mind, putting you
back on your feet and down the road to recovery.

You turn the pamphlet over; on the back it says, "For more information, please contact the Sunnydale Suicide Prevention Society (SSPS)," with an address and phone number listed. Also on the desk are a few papers and a notebook that the counselor appears to have been working from. You rifle through the papers before noticing one placed squarely in the center of the desk, weighed down by a man's signet ring with a crescent moon insignia on it. Your gaze travels down to the words at the end of the letter:

I'm so sorry to let you all down. I can't fight it
anymore, and this is the only way I know how to
stop it. Do not let it get to you, too.

That's odd. Wasn't this just about the same choice of words Diana Fitzgerald used in *her* suicide note?

You let your attention turn toward the spiral-bound notebook on the edge of the desk, with "Doug Teal" scribbled on the front cover. Upon opening it, you discover it contains notes belonging to the grief counselor detailing his previous appointments with students. Rapidly flipping through the pages, you see the names of other schools listed, including one in a town called Vera Icon, before coming across today's appointments at Sunnydale High.

"Right this way, gentlemen. He's working with

our students out of my office." The familiar gruff strains of Principal Snyder's voice echo down the hallway outside. You take one last look at the man in the khakis hanging from the ceiling fan—*nice pants,* you think morosely—and realize that if you don't get out of the office but quick, Snyder's going to see you standing there behind his desk, the dead man's papers spread out before you, and have you arrested in a heartbeat. With your record, going back to your days in L.A. when you burned down your old school's gymnasium, the authorities aren't likely to take into account your version of events. Best to hightail it out of there.

With lightning speed you pitch yourself at the window, slide it open, and are about to dive out when you realize you have just enough time to grab one of the items belonging to the grief counselor off the desk before Snyder walks through the door. But which will help you most in your potential investigation?

SLAYER CHOICE:

Do you decide to . . .

❚ take the suicide note? *If yes, turn to page 96.*

❚ take the spiral-bound notebook? *If yes, turn to page 17.*

You grab the notebook and dive out the window, clearing the sill just as Principal Snyder swings open the door to his office. "Good lord," you hear him exclaim, his tone not so very different from the one he uses to issue his usual stern warnings. "Get me the Mayor's office on the phone," he barks, most likely to his assistant cowering in the hallway.

Crawling a safe distance away from the open window, you stand and head toward the side of the building, where you sit on the edge of the courtyard fountain to peruse your stolen booty: the grief counselor's spiral-bound notebook.

The first page has "Clearview HS, Santa Cruz, CA" written and underlined across the top. Below is a series of names and dates; as you read, they begin to take on a chilling significance.

Marcus Johnson, 16 d. Jan. 4
Daniel Getty, 18 d. Jan. 9
Francine de Soto, 18 d. Jan. 14
Sam Messner, 15 d. Jan. 17
Regina Lunt, 46 (teacher) d. Jan. 17

Then, nothing. On the opposite page, however, is a new set of names, with notes beneath each one. You soon realize that they are notes the grief counselor took during his appointments. Not just with students, you read, but teachers as well. The meeting with the first Clearview High student is dated January 18, the day after the last death. In other words, when the grief counselor came to the school, the apparent suicides ceased. *Most impressive,* you think.

You turn the page—another high school in another town is listed, with another set of names and dates, this time longer and starting more than a month later. On the opposite page again are notes from the counselor's appointments with the students and faculty. Again, the deaths stopped abruptly after the appearance of the grief counselor.

What gives? Aside from the fact that this looks like some kind of assassin's hit list, what's particularly strange is the way the deaths are so tightly clustered, a phenomenon that continues in the subsequent entries. Whether or not these are actual suicides, whatever it is rolls into town, makes a killing, then takes off. Easy in, easy out. Only not so easy for those left in its wake.

You flip to the back of the notebook, past some blank pages at the end, and before a similar entry on a high school in the town of Vera Icon, you find written:

> Sunnydale HS, Sunnydale, CA
> Madison Collins, 17 d. Sept. 20
> Barbara O'Hearn, 18 d. Oct. 9
> Darren Blank, 18 d. Oct. 17
> Diana Fitzgerald, 17 d. Oct. 20

That's interesting: The last three students on the list supposedly killed themselves, but Madison, who was in your history class, died of an allergic reaction to peanuts he accidentally ate on a camping trip with his brother. Didn't he? And now, of course, there was a new name to be added: Doug Teal, grief counselor.

On the opposite page, dated today, are his final appointment notes. Since school let out less than an hour ago, only four names appear: Ricky Watts, Carter Bowens, Jonathan Levenson, and . . . Oh, yeah. Right. Buffy Summers.

Then that thought, that all-too-familiar nagging thought hits you: *Maybe if I'd showed up a little earlier, I could have stopped this from happening. . . .*

But no. You have to put the kibosh on such negativity. This type of thinking never helped save lives in the past, and it sure as hell isn't going to start performing CPR on anyone anytime soon. So you stare at the page again and wonder what to do next. One option is to find the last person who saw Mr. Teal alive. According to the list, that would be Jonathan Levenson, that kinda harmless, nerdy kid who always seems to be popping up. The appointment notes under his name say, "Smart, top student, sensitive, signs of depression," then, "Possibly serious?"

Wow, the student body really isn't making with the glass half full, is it? Not that part of you can't relate; you've been feeling pretty teen angsty yourself lately. Angel's been in full brood mode for the past few weeks, your mom's constantly disappointed in you, and your classes . . . well, let's just say you're not going to win any school-spirit awards in the near future.

You flip back a few pages, to the record of alleged suicides. Madison Collins—why is he listed here when he died accidentally? Did the grief counselor know something you don't? It may be time to pay a belated condolence call to Madison's family and see what you can dig up.

The only other thing in the notebook to really grab on to is something tucked into its pages. It's a piece of stationery, with the your school's address scribbled on it. The letterhead, however, is for the Westmoreland House. You know that place; it's a little bed-and-breakfast not so far from school, where your father was planning on staying during a weekend visit, until he bailed on you, as per usual. It's possible something in Mr. Teal's room will tell you more about his travels from high school to high school, and why the suicide clusters always seemed to stop upon his arrival.

SLAYER CHOICE:

Do you decide to . . .

❚ talk to Jonathan Levenson, the grief counselor's final appointment and presumably the last person to see him alive? *If yes, turn to page 21.*

❚ pay a belated condolence call to Madison Collins's family to find out more about his supposed accident? *If yes, turn to page 140.*

❚ drop by the bed-and-breakfast for the skinny on Mr. Teal's past? *If yes, turn to page 66.*

You look through the window on the door of the *Sentinel,* the Sunnydale High student newspaper, and see Jonathan Levenson, his compact frame hunched over a typewriter, pounding away on the keys. You knock and watch him jump, then catch his breath before waving you in.

"Hey, Jonathan, what's up?"

"Nothing much. You startled me. I was just doing a little writing," he says, nodding in the direction of the positively antique-looking Smith-Corona.

"Wow, I didn't think anyone still used those. Not even electric, huh? Is that still legal?"

"Barely," he replies, smiling. "Makes checking your e-mail a little difficult."

"I can imagine. So, you working on something for the paper?"

"Uh, no, actually." He leans back slightly, obscuring your view of the page in the typewriter. "Nothing special. Just some . . . creative writing."

"Mind if I take a look?"

"Actually, it's sort of private. Sorry, Buffy. It's more like a journal entry than anything else. A way to get my feelings out."

"Is that something the grief counselor suggested?"

"Yeah, it is. Did he ask you to do the same thing?"

"No. No, he didn't. Jonathan, can I ask you about your meeting with Mr. Teal?"

"Sure. What do you want to know?"

"Everything. If it's not too personal, that is. What I really want to know about is Mr. Teal. What did he say? Did he seem troubled to you in any way?"

"Funny you should mention it," Jonathan replies, now less nervous and more relieved to be sharing his disconcernment. "At first, he just seemed sort of distracted and, I don't know, preoccupied, I guess, like he had something else on his mind. So, he started asking me questions, like, how's my home life, things like that. He had my transcript with him, and wanted to know how my classes were going, extracurriculars, what I do outside of school. He also asked me if I knew any of the kids who killed themselves, and what I thought about it, and if I ever thought about doing something like that myself. I told him I was lonely sometimes, and sad, but . . . that's all I said."

"And? *Did* you know any of the others who died?"

"Not really. I mean, Darren took pictures for the *Sentinel* sometimes, and we worked on a few features together, but that's about it. But the grief counselor . . . There was something not quite right with him. I mean, besides seeming distracted."

"What do you mean?"

"Well, it was strange. I was in the middle of telling him about how my parents keep saying that they'll only pay for college if I go to an Ivy League school, and how I really want to go to Stanford, and"—Jonathan senses your attention waning and jumps to the good stuff—"he started to change. He got this funny faraway look in his eyes. It was like he was concentrating really hard—listening, even—only it wasn't to me. He was tuned in to a different channel."

"Then what happened?"

"He told me to write something down—what I was feeling, I guess. At least, I think that's what he said. It was hard to tell because he started mumbling, and it was hard to understand. Then it seemed like he was just talking to himself, something about running out of time, life being short. He kept fidgeting, too—rubbing his hands together, taking his ring off and putting it back on, rifling through his papers." He stops then and gives you a suspicious glance. "Why are you asking me about all this, anyway?"

"Let's just say something bad happened."

"Really bad?"

"We're talking *Gigli* bad. Did Mr. Teal say anything else?"

"There *was* something else. He said something like, 'I can't stop you.' Or maybe it was 'It can't be stopped.'"

"That's it?"

"That's all I can remember."

"Thanks, Jonathan. You've been a big help."

You walk out of the *Sentinel* offices and shut the door behind you, listening to the sound of distant laughter echoing through the school's emptied hallways at day's end. Something—or someone—*made* Mr. Teal kill himself. Demon possession? Power of suggestion? Severe acute depression? The possibilities are wide open.

Time to make a move. You can put your ear to the street and see what you come up with there. Why not shake down some demon haunts, vamp nests, and the like? After all, it's amazing how talkative some creatures become with a broadsword to their necks. And you know just the place to start: Willy's bar, the sleazy spot frequented by all kinds of things that go bump in the night, or, in this case, bump in the happy hour. If anyone already knows something bad is in town, it's probably Willy the Snitch himself.

Another option is to check in on Willow; always eager to be deputized on another Slayer mission, she could use her computer skills to hack into state and federal records, which might prove to be helpful in any number of ways. You could learn about Mr. Teal and the path the suicides took across California, or, if these deaths weren't caused by something supernatural, what other explanations could possibly exist.

SLAYER CHOICE:

Do you decide to . . .

❚ go to Willow's house and see what she can dig up online about Mr. Teal and the pattern of suicides? *If yes, turn to page 147.*

❚ hit Willy's bar and scare up some information the painful way? *If yes, turn to page 25.*

Willy's place is packed with the usual happy-hour crowd—demons, early-bird vampires, and, judging from the appearance of some seriously skanky-looking creatures at the end of the bar, possibly a few succubi as well. Willy, cleaning a mug behind the bar with a dirty dish towel, looks up at you and does a double take, then proceeds to let the glass slip from his hands. As it crashes to the floor, everyone in the bar looks to Willy, then transfers their gaze to you; a few vamps get up from their stools and take their drinks to the back of the room. Attempting to strike a casual pose beside the cash register but unable to remain still, Willy is doing a very poor job of disguising his fear and consternation at your presence. You wouldn't have it any other way, though, and enjoy the surge of confidence that fills you as you slowly approach the countertop.

"Ah, uh, a good evening to you, *Slayer,*" Willy says, causing a few heads to raise, horned and otherwise. "What can I get you to drink?"

"Honestly? You couldn't get me to drink anything in this place," you say, your eyes quickly shifting to take in the macabre array of beverages lining the shelves behind him; at least one bottle appears to be looking back at you. "The last time I was in here, I saw some guy order a virgin Bloody Mary, and . . . well, you know."

"So, you, uh, didn't drop by for a drink, then," Willy says nervously, the back of his hand wiping sweat from his brow.

"Nope. Not even here for the oh-so-romantic

ambience." You glare over at the other end of the bar. "I came for some information."

"I don't know nothing about nobody, Slayer. I swear."

"Your double negative says otherwise. Why don't you start by telling me about the new power in town?"

"And who might that be?"

"Oh, I dunno. Demonish. Likes to travel. Has a soft spot for staging suicides."

"Suicides?" Willy's eyes go wide. "What kind of self-respecting demon would go and do a thing like that?"

"That's what I want to know. What do you hear?"

"This is the first of it. If I hear anything, I'll be sure to tell you. Anyway, gotta get back to my customers, so you have yourself a nice—"

Before he has a chance to finish his sentence, you reach out, grab his head with both hands, and slam it down onto the countertop, smashing the side of his face just hard enough to scare him.

"Ow! What'd you do that for?" His hand goes up to his cheek and holds it delicately. "I told you, I don't know nothing."

You grasp his head once more, this time sending the other side of his face into the bar, accompanied by a loud cracking sound. "I can do this all day, Willy. And I got to tell you, I'm finding it strangely relaxing. Now, unless you'd like me to find a few more places on your head to tenderize, I suggest you start getting your chat on."

Willy shakes you off, then adjusts his shirt, now twisted and stretched out around the collar. He eyes his patrons, who are now visibly uneasy in your presence but are busily pretending not to watch you shake him down.

You cross your arms, waiting. Finally Willy leans forward conspiratorially and whispers, "Okay, I may have picked up a little something from some Miquot demons who were in here a couple of days ago."

"What did you hear?"

"Something big just arrived in town, and it's setting up camp. Really old, really evil. Something that can't be stopped."

You roll your eyes. "If I had a nickel for every time I've heard about something old and evil that can't be stopped, I'd—well, I'd have about a dollar fifty."

"Those Miquots didn't sound so happy about it. They're staying down by the docks if you want to know more."

"You got anything else? A name? An address? A license plate number in ancient Sumerian?"

"No, but I can tell you you're not the first person today to march in here and start asking me about suicide."

"Someone was poking around, asking about a new player?"

"No, not that, just about, you know, my feelings. Whether I know people who're depressed or want to kill themselves, stuff like that."

"Who was it? Tall, thin guy? Balding?" Could it have been the grief counselor, before he came to school for his scheduled student appointments?

"Nope. It was some chick. Mousylike. Buttoned-up

cardigan, schoolmarm bun, little string of pearls. I thought she was hawking the *Watchtower* or something. But she said she was canvassing as part of a new mental-health survey. Here," he said, reaching behind the bar. "She left me this."

He hands you a postcard-size flyer. On the front, set on a navy background, are the words *Feeling Blue?* in bold white lettering. The back reads, *We know how to help you. Come on in to our new crisis treatment center for a free and confidential evaluation, and start out on the road to recovery today.* On the bottom the organization's name, Sunnydale Suicide Prevention Society, is listed with an address and telephone number.

Well, you think, *at least somebody seems concerned about what's going on in this town.* You remember seeing the SSPS pamphlets on Snyder's desk, alongside Mr. Teal's other things. Was Mr. Teal working with them to stop the wave of student suicides? Also, if they were canvassing places of business around town, could that mean the rash of deaths cuts a wider swath than you previously thought?

You thank Willy by not hitting him again and step out into the crisp autumn air as night begins to settle all around you. What to do, what to do . . . You can go see about these Miquot demons at the docks and find out what's up with this "really old, really evil" talk. Then there's always this Sunnydale Suicide Prevention Society; it's getting late and they may be closed by now, but they might be able to help you with some of your questions. If anyone knows about the state of the town's current suicide problem, it's probably them.

Then again, you don't exactly have the whole evening off to go Nancy Drewing after some deaths that, tragic as they are, may not even *be* supernatural in nature. This is a bad time to be neglecting your duties as Slayer, which means the same thing it always does: patrolling. *Angel's always game for that,* you think. *Insert sigh here.*

You turn up your collar and start down the street, feeling the weight of the stake in your jacket pocket tapping steadily against you with your stride. Another evening on the Hellmouth. You can barely contain your enthusiasm.

SLAYER CHOICE:

Do you decide to . . .

❚ go to the docks and look for the Miquot demons to see if you can get any info on the new evil in town? *If yes, turn to page 64.*

❚ head to the Sunnydale Suicide Prevention Society for some answers about the rash of suicides? *If yes, turn to page 30.*

❚ get patrolling and fight evil the old-fashioned way: by staking vamps and making out with Angel? *If yes, turn to page 109.*

You make your way up the narrow path of stones to the front of the gargantuan Victorian-style mansion, the last house on the street, with SUNNYDALE SUICIDE PREVENTION SOCIETY stenciled on a sign out front. Stepping up on the porch, you can see that most of the downstairs lights are off, but there's still a soft glow emanating from somewhere within. Up on your toes, you try to peer in through the small windows high up on the door, but your view of the long hallway beyond is largely obscured by the darkness and the translucent curtains. You knock, then wait a few moments before knocking again, harder this time. A bright light comes on somewhere down the hall, and soon a woman appears, in her twenties maybe, hurrying to open the door.

"Oh, hello, dear," she says upon seeing you. "I'm so sorry, but we just closed for the evening. Is everything all right? Do you want to talk with someone?"

You try to take her in without obviously looking her up and down. She's dressed primly for such a young woman, wearing a cardigan over a frilly white blouse, a thin string of pearls, and glasses.

"No, nothing like that," you say. "I was just looking for some information. For school. I'm writing a research paper on . . . teen suicides."

"You must be concerned about what happened to some of your fellow students," she says, nodding sympathetically. "Well, if you hear of anyone who's not doing so well emotionally, you make sure you send them here, and we can get them the help they need."

"Thanks, I'll do that. So, you guys are new in town, huh?"

"Yes, we've been here just a few days now."

"Awfully good timing, what with all these suicides happening all of a sudden."

"Yes, well, we go where we're needed." You sense an uncomfortable ripple in the air between you.

"So . . . where were you before you came to Sunnydale?"

"Oh, we're something of a nomadic organization. We've set up shop in many cities and towns all across the country."

"And where were you last?"

"We just came from a sleepy little town up the coast called Vera Icon. Cutest place. Outside of Crescent City, near the Oregon border."

Vera Icon . . . That sounds familiar, but you're not sure why exactly. "Do you by any chance know a grief counselor who works with high school students? I think he may have traveled around a lot himself. Doug Teal?"

You watch the unmistakable shadow of recognition pass over her face—faint, but definitely there—before her expression returns to a kind of stony cheerfulness. "Sorry, dear, I don't know anyone by that name. Why, is that who they brought in to the local high school to meet with you kids?"

"Yes, he just showed up this morning. I . . . saw him just a couple of hours ago."

"And did he answer all your questions?"

"No, not so much. He's—well—he's dead, actually."

"My lord!" she exclaims. Her hand goes up to cover her open mouth, but her eyes, wide with surprise, nevertheless sparkle with nervous excitement. "Whatever happened to him?"

"Well, surprisingly, it looks like he killed himself. He was hanging from the ceiling by his necktie."

"Goodness me!" *Goodness me?* you think. *Is she for real?* "Did you see him like that, dear?"

"Yes, yes, I did," you say, attempting to feign a suitably traumatized tone of voice—hollow, confused, on the verge of choking up. "It was awful. I can't get the image out of my head." *If she only knew,* you think. *Nobody knows the bodies I've seen,* you hum in your head.

"Maybe it would be best if you came in after all," the woman says expectantly. "I could fetch you something to drink, and we could . . . talk."

You wanted inside this place, and now here's your entrée. . . . But suddenly you're not so sure. There's something off about this woman: her creepy mannerisms, her buttoned-up outfit, her weird diction. You can totally picture this as the penultimate scene in *Buffy the Movie,* costarring Kathy Bates as Suicide Lady, complete with a small but critical cameo by a sledgehammer currently resting against the wall on the other side of the door.

Then again, maybe you're being unfair. So she's

kind of odd, but she probably means well. She's concerned for your well-being. Not everyone you run into who looks square and acts friendly toward you is going to turn out to be a psycho killer. Right?

SLAYER CHOICE:
Do you decide to . . .

❚ take up the Sunnydale Suicide Prevention Society worker on her kind offer of tea and sympathy? *If yes, turn to page 101.*

❚ beg off and say you best be heading home, then secretly double back to do some snooping around the property? *If yes, turn to page 34.*

Standing on the porch of the Sunnydale Suicide Prevention Society, you realize that maybe it's not such a good idea to spend any after-hours time with the woman who answered the door. You're not sure if it's intuition or merely a paranoid aversion to people who seem too nice to be sincere, but whatever it is, you're not going to go inside with her. "I'm really sorry, but it's getting late and I should get home before my mom starts worrying. She's really freaked out about all these kids who died."

"All right," the woman says. "As long as you're sure you're okay?"

"Okay? Okay's my middle name!" you say with a bit too much pep. "I mean, it *would* be, if it wasn't Anne. So, I'll just come back tomorrow when you're open and pick up some literature then. Have a nice night!"

"You too, dear. Take care now." You head back down the stone pathway and out onto the sidewalk. The woman remains standing in the doorway; you can practically feel the heat from her gaze on the back of your neck as you make your way down the block, turning at the corner.

Once you're out of view, you duck down behind the high row of hedges surrounding the property and double back—no way are you going to pass up a chance to do some reconnaissance. Nightfall has provided you just enough cover to make your way unseen through the wall of hedges and around the side of the tall, narrow mansion that houses the SSPS. Keeping low, you scuttle across the lawn, avoiding the brightly lit squares cast on the grass from a row of windows high on the third floor. When you reach the rear wall of the building, you carefully peer in through the nearest window.

Inside, barely visible by the dim light from the hall-way, you see the woman who answered the door. She's standing beside a long table covered in books and papers—you can just make out the tabletop from this low angle. Sitting on the other side of the table is a man in his twenties in a corduroy jacket with elbow patches, old-fashioned suspenders on slacks that manage to be both high-water and high-waisted, and a shirt buttoned all the way up to his neck—he looks like he's twenty-five going on eighty. As did his colleague, actually, the woman now speaking to him in rapid-fire but inaudible words, her arms flailing wildly. You can't hear what they're discussing, but whatever it is, it looks important.

You look up at the windows on the top floor. The light from inside is bright but inconstant, almost mes-merizing in the way it waxes and wanes in intensity against the windows' paper-thin curtains. There's something going on up there—time to get a better view.

There's a fire escape on the back of the building; you overturn a garbage can to give you an extra two feet of height, in order to jump up and grab the bottom rung of the retractable ladder. Pulling yourself to the first landing, you silently creep up the steps, mak-ing your way to the roof before lowering yourself down onto a small balcony attached to the eerily illu-minated room at the front of the mansion. Keeping flat against the outside of the window frame, you crouch down and crane your neck to see inside the room.

Oh boy. Arranged in a candlelit circle are ten, maybe twelve, figures cloaked in dark brown robes, each face obscured by a long cowl that hangs down over the nose; it looks almost like an abbreviated veil. Atop these sleek hoods are stitched narrow golden eyes as if to replicate those of a snake. The way the candlelight dances across the embroidery makes it seem like the eyes are alive and in motion, searching out prey.

The door to the room opens, and you watch as the man and woman from downstairs enter, each taking a robe from one of the pegs on the far wall. They slip into the dark robes, pull the hoods down over their faces, and join the group. You lean forward, trying to get a look at what's on the altar beside the circle, but your view is partially blocked; all you can see are a few items, including an ivory-handled broadsword, a small wooden box, and a scroll rolled up on both ends.

The dozen or so assembled take hands then, raising their arms above their heads, and in unison begin a low, menacing chant. *"Dark K'adolh, King K'adolh, we bring you forth. Dark K'adolh, King K'adolh."* Soon a strange sensation begins to creep into the air, an undercurrent of electricity—you can feel it buzzing in your ears, even on the other side of the window. You start to get the feeling it's about time for your leavetaking when the hooded figures inside begin to rotate counterclockwise, revealing a lone figure on her knees in the center of the circle.

"Willow!" you gasp. She's shivering with fright, desperately scrambling backward to the side of the ring to stay as far from the broadsword on the altar as possible. As she thrashes against them, you see that she has her hands tied behind her back with thick copper wire. And now you've seen enough.

You lean back before pitching yourself forward, crashing through the large windows bracketing the balcony. Rolling along the floor, you right yourself beside the altar where, with one fluid gesture, you slide the broadsword from its sheath and pull it back behind your head. For a split second you consider yelling something along the lines of, "Now, step away from the redhead," but if the big pointy sword in your hand isn't enough to clue them in, there's not much else to say. So instead you swing the blade, sending people ducking for cover in every direction, leaving Willow by herself in the center of the room. You kick over a candelabra heavy with candles, and a powdery substance, possibly incense, strewn across the wooden floorboards the length of the room goes up in rows of blue fire. Willow is barely visible in the steady stream of smoke now thickening the air, sweetening it with the smell of wet birch and primrose.

"Buffy!" she shouts, motioning toward her bound arms, which you free by cutting through the wire with a swift and sure arc of the sword. One of the hooded figures regains his daring and lunges at you, but you swing him around, using his own weight to send him crashing out the window, the panes of which have already been liberated of their glass by your dramatic entrance. Two more approach to attack you from behind, but you're too quick, pivoting and delivering a roundhouse kick that sends one careening into the other, taking a tapestry down from the wall in the process.

Now there's a clear path between you and the door; you don't have a second to waste. "Go!" you shout at Willow, who, staying low, covers her mouth and dives through the wall of smoke toward freedom. Suddenly someone hits you from behind, knocking you back against the altar, which topples over, spraying its contents across the burning floor. Right next to you fall two of the things you previously noticed on the altar, only this time you have a much better look at them. One is a smallish wooden box, emblazoned with the image of a crescent moon, and the other is a scroll that looks seriously ancient, like if you sneezed on it something really ancient and butt-ugly would fly out of it like at the end of *Raiders of the Lost Ark*. Unfortunately you only have time to grab one of them before following Willow out the door and away from the burning building, ostensibly to safety.

SLAYER CHOICE:

Do you decide to . . .

❚ grab the moon box on your way out the door? *If yes, turn to page 145.*

❚ take the scroll instead? *If yes, turn to page 39.*

"**M**ost interesting." Giles hasn't lifted his head from the light box's magnification lens in the five full minutes since he asked you to kill the lights. The library, in near total darkness, has taken on a distinctly ominous air. You never feel completely safe here after nightfall as it is, tonight even less so, despite the fact that with Xander, Cordelia, you, Willow, and Giles gathered nervously around the long study table, this is as close to a heavily populated area as the school library ever gets.

"What's most interesting?" you say, looking from Giles to Willow and back. You've never seen her in such rough shape, which is saying a lot at this point in your Hellmouth-infused friendship. In fact, she's barely said a word since you rescued her. First she was freaked by the grief counselor's death, then the creepiness at the Sunnydale Suicide Prevention Society, where she was held captive by a bunch of . . . well, who were they, anyway?

"The Order of Shifrah," Giles says, his eyes still glued to the scroll beneath the glass.

"That's who those snaky people were?"

"That's the group to whom the creation of this scroll is attributed, which doesn't necessarily make them the . . . 'snaky people.' One moment." Giles goes behind the circulation desk and into his office, quickly surfacing with a stack of various musty tomes that he proceeds to leaf through with wild abandon while murmuring to himself. "*The Schiller-Aptekar Grimoire* . . . no . . . Perhaps the *Book of Thoth* . . . That's not it. . . . *Weiron's Codex* . . . yes . . . What about—*aha!*" he exclaims loudly, causing Xander to jump in his seat. Giles triumphantly displays a book bound in red leather by holding it over his head and pivoting from side to side, to the excitement of no one but himself, before sheepishly lowering it and returning to the relevant passage. He adjusts his spectacles on the bridge of his nose and begins to read aloud.

"'The Order of Shifrah is a sect primarily associated with sorcery and mysticism, whose origins date back at least to the time of the pharaoh Amenhotep I in ancient Egypt. The order, which first consisted of a small coven of witches enslaved by the pharaoh, was initially formed as a secret investigatory body to examine a disturbing epidemic: that of a suspected suicide contagion among the slaves.'"

"Because usually it's such a breeze being a slave to the pharaoh," Xander interjects. "I mean, those pyramids, they practically build themselves."

Giles gives him an obligatory disapproving glance before continuing. "'What they discovered was that the pronounced suicide rate was caused by the arrival in their midst of a demon known as K'adolh, who dwelt along the riverbanks of the Nile, feeding off the misery of the enslaved. The Order of Shifrah managed to render K'adolh incorporeal, caging his essence within a papyrus leaf on which the binding spell is written.'" Your Watcher walks back over to the light box and slides the scroll out from under the magnification lens. "This scroll has all of the appropriate identifying markings. It must be the original paper that trapped the demon."

"Well, if the Big, Bad, and Depressing is stuck inside the paper," you ask, eyeing him as he handles the scroll, "then what exactly is going on?"

"'The demon,'" Giles continues, putting the scroll down and returning to the text, "'though physically powerless, escaped by entering the body of a human host, one of the pharaoh's guards who unwittingly seized the papyrus following a raid on the Order of Shifrah's makeshift temple. K'adolh then ripened the host from within by implanting dark thoughts in his mind and feeding off the resulting melancholia.

"'For sustenance K'adolh must move from person to person, jumping to the next host using paper as his conduit, leaving before his victim ends his or her own life. And so, it is said, K'adolh travels, continent to continent, throughout the ages, passing from hand to hand via the last piece of paper touched, be it a suicide note, a book, a bus ticket. As legend has it, K'adolh's best-known method of infection, a playing card, earned the king of hearts the nickname "the Suicide King." To this day the figure on this card is almost always depicted as a king putting a sword to his own head.'"

"If there's anything about a murderous old maid in there," Xander says, "I don't want to know."

"What's he looking for?" you ask. "What does he want?" Cordelia gets up from where she's sitting and stands beside Giles, looking over his shoulder at the scroll.

"I'm not entirely sure, but I suspect that the 'snaky people'—that is, the apparent occult group operating

under the auspices of the suicide prevention society—
are planning something much greater." He places the
open book on the table, the pages turned to a disturbing
etching of a circle of demon worshippers clad in the
skins of snakes. "The Cult of K'adolh, recognizable by
the sign of the *Naja haje,* or Egyptian cobra. The mortal enemies of the Order of Shifrah, the Cult of
K'adolh seeks to recorporealize their demon king. If I
had to venture a guess, I would posit that they are planning on using the confluence of mystical energies that
is the Hellmouth to achieve their goal."

"So, anyway, now that the cult is out of commis-
sion, thanks to little miss arsonist here," Cordy says,
waving a dismissive hand in your direction, "what's
the next step? I mean, how are you supposed to go
about finding a shapeless, formless suicide demon that
jumps from person to person?"

Giles turns to Cordy and says, "Oh, I don't imagine it will prove very difficult." With that, in one fluid
motion, he extends an arm, flicking the ancient scroll
of the Order of Shifrah down the long length of the
study table. Instinctively Willow, seated at the end of
the table, puts out her hands to catch it.

When she makes contact with the scroll, a violent
wave of white electricity rips through the room
before pulling back on itself, contracting. Xander
backs away from the table where Willow now sits
alone, illuminated, her eyes glowing a shimmering,
serpentine gold.

"So good of you to show yourself," Giles says,

stepping between Willow and Cordy, whose eyes are wide with fear.

You watch your best friend's eyes slowly narrow, her lips curling up into a sinister smile. *"K'ADOLH,"* she says, in a deep and booming voice so very far from her own. *"YOU MAY CALL ME K'ADOLH."*

SLAYER ACTION:
Turn to page 44.

"**H**ow's it going?" you ask, kneeling down beside Giles, who is busy drawing Nordic protection runes on the floor of the library in chalk.

"About as well as can be expected," he replies. "Jenny, any progress?"

"In fits and spurts, mostly." The newly arrived Jenny Calendar, your Watcher's on-again girlfriend, the Sunnydale High computer instructor and self-described technopagan, is currently behind the circulation desk, combing through one of Giles's books. "The bulk of this stuff is really outdated, Rupert. Surely there's an updated version of this devocation ritual. I mean, 'Two pinches of warlock's vein?' I don't think it's even politically correct to use the word 'warlock' anymore, let alone pinch his vein."

"Forgive me, Ms. Calendar. Perhaps you could find a more handicapable version of that eighteenth-century exorcism manual somewhere online."

"Maybe I could, if you ever got around to upgrading your Internet subscription databases. God forbid, in a high school library . . . ," she says, singsonging the last words under her breath.

It never ceases to amaze you how those around you always fall back on familiar banter and humor in an effort to avoid the five-hundred-pound gorilla in the middle of the room—or, in this case, the hundred-twenty-pound, demon-possessed girl tied to a chair in the middle of the room. Although it—he? she?—is increasingly difficult to ignore, as it is gradually becoming ever more vocal.

"YOU DARE TO CONSTRAIN K'ADOLH?" it

bellows through the mouth of Willow, its eyes glowing gold with fury and split with a serpent's narrow red pupils. *"YOU WHO WOULD CONSPIRE TO DESTROY MY MINIONS AND PREVENT MY INEVITABLE DOMINION OVER THIS PLANE, RELEASE THE MORTAL VESSEL FROM THESE SHACKLES AND I WILL MAKE YOUR DEATHS QUICK. OTHERWISE, YOUR DEMISE WILL BE EXCRUCIATING. I WILL TAKE EXACTING PLEASURE IN RENDING YOUR FLESH FROM ITS BONE, TASTING EACH SWEET AGONY AS YOUR BLOOD SPILLS FROM ITS FLESHY CASKETS, GORGING ON—"*

"You might kill us first by boring us to death," Cordelia shouts from Giles's office. "For an hour now you've been going *on* and *on* and *on* about blood this and vessel that. Somebody please hit the snooze bar already!" She comes out with a box of magick supplies and slams it down on the table. "And could you *be* a little louder? My head is *pounding*. Why, oh, why, I ask you, do demons always have to talk in ALL CAPS?"

"FEEBLE CHILD," it spits, craning Willow's head in Cordelia's direction. *"I, K'ADOLH, BRINGER OF DESPAIR AND SELF-INFLICTED DOOM TO LEGIONS, WILL NOT BE MOCKED LIGHTLY. FOR AS SURELY AS THE ASP TAKES DARK PLEASURE IN DEVOURING THE PREY THAT SUSTAINS IT, SO TOO SHALL I RELISH CONSUMING YOUR PATHETIC SOUL UNTIL YOU'RE BEGGING TO END IT ALL."*

"I can't believe I'm about to say this," Cordy pronounces, turning her back on K'adolh and visibly struggling to remain calm, "but I'm actually starting to miss the old Willow."

"Buffy, before we do this," Giles says, his soft voice almost a whisper in your head, "I want to make sure that you're aware, fully aware, of the consequences."

"Aware, Giles?" you say, turning to look into his sad eyes. "What does that even mean? That I'm sufficiently racked with guilt by deciding on behalf of my best friend that she may have to die in order to kill this demon and save humanity?"

"Whatever we do, it has to be done now. We don't know how strong the Cult of K'adolh's forces are—he's becoming desperate and could make a move that will permanently harm Willow."

"So what are our choices? Undertake the exorcism, which will kill K'adolh and possibly Willow along with him? Or don't perform the ritual, which may buy us some time to find another way to safely extract the demon, but may cause her even more damage the longer she's possessed?"

"In a nutshell, yes," Giles replies. "Those are your choices."

"Actually," Jenny Calendar says, stepping out from behind the circulation counter, "there's one more option."

"I'm all ears," you say.

"The corporealization spell that K'adolh's followers were attempting to perform. I think I can figure out how to replicate it, and it should release the demon from Willow's body without causing her any harm."

"Are you mad?" Giles scoffs. "If K'adolh is powerful enough in his incorporeal form to cause such rampant destruction, we can't even begin to fathom the power at his disposal once we birth him into physical existence. We could be dead within minutes. This entire town could be under his control by daybreak."

As you listen to Giles and Ms. Calendar argue, your gaze travels from Xander's panic-stricken grimace to Willow's face, so familiar to you but now twisted into some kind of horrible death mask, her mouth stretched into a cruel sneer, daring you to make a decision. You don't want to wait to act.

Destroy K'adolh, and possibly Willow.

Save Willow, thereby bringing the demon into the world, possibly killing you, your friends, and all of humanity.

The choice is yours.

SLAYER CHOICE:

Do you decide to . . .

❘ go through with the exorcism ritual and devoke K'adolh? *If yes, turn to page 134.*

❘ perform the corporealization spell to restore K'adolh? *If yes, turn to page 48.*

"We call forth K'adolh, King of Despair." It's hard to believe, but here you are, alongside your friends, birthing a demon into the world. *This may be a new low,* you think, *but it's the only way to be sure Willow won't be harmed.* You've made your decision. What happens next, however, is anyone's guess.

"Come forward," your Watcher continues, "and step into this mortal plane." You, Giles, Jenny Calendar, Xander, and Cordelia are each holding a black candle and standing at one point on the pentagram crudely chalked onto the library floor, with Willow, still tied to the chair, at its center. Giles blows out his candle, and the demon hisses through Willow's lips as it is slowly being wrenched out of her.

"We beseech thee, Demon Lord, walk amongst us once more," Cordelia says, her nerves finally starting to show, "and take your rightful place on the throne of all creation." She blows out her candle and the air begins to crackle with golden electricity.

"Leave your prison of flesh," Ms. Calendar intones, sprinkling some excess powdered incense on her candle's flame, "and join your subjects in the waking world." She extinguishes her candle with two fingers, and smoke begins to rise from Willow's flesh; a long, continuous scream escapes her lips.

"Giles, what's happening to her?" you shout over the din, but he silences you with a finger to his lips. Xander runs his empty hand over his hair—all the blood seems to have rushed from his face, but he manages to press on, taking a moment to recall his part of the ritual.

"Your time is now, your time is always. . . . Lead

us into the darkening hour." He blows out his candle, and Willow is silenced as a glowing wraithlike form floats into the air above her. It's not fully formed but flickering, here one moment and gone the next, a translucent humanoid shape stretched out from head to foot, a long mane of hair whipping back and forth like a snake struggling to free itself from a predator's grasp.

"Dark K'adolh, King K'adolh, we bring you forth." You can barely get the words out. On top of your foot rests a battle-ax, ready to be snapped up in an instant and hurled at K'adolh once he's fully materialized. But will it be enough?

"Dark K'adolh, King K'adolh," you continue, the air positively alive with unholy energy, "show us yourself in all your infinite glory."

With that, you blow out the candle, and, save one last burst of light and fire, the library is pitched into total darkness.

"Xander, the lights!" you scream, kicking your foot up, the ax snapping into your hand.

"They're not working! They're . . ." And then you hear him shriek, as if a thousand nails are driving into him, followed by a choking sound. You leap across the ritual area, over where you imagine Willow still sits tied to the chair, and collide headlong into Xander, knocking him over. You reach down in the dark and feel the tightness of his chest, his arms, his hands . . . which are clutching his own throat, busily suffocating himself.

You try to pry his hands off, to no avail; not even

your Slayer strength can seem to budge them. Then, on the other side of the room, Cordelia gasps, accompanied by a loud smashing noise. *No. This is not really happening. No . . .*

You release Xander's arms, take a deep breath, then punch him in the side of the head, just hard enough to render him unconscious. Okay. That's a start.

Something brushes by you, knocking you on your back. You flip up, and just then Giles shouts, "Close your eyes!" before the sound of glass breaking ruptures the eerie stillness of the dark.

"Everybody down!" you order, accompanied by the dull thump of bodies hitting the floor. This is it. Only one chance to act, one choice left . . .

You close your eyes, leaping into the air, spinning, and release the battle-ax, guided by nothing more than intuition and adrenaline.

You hear a sharp *thwack!* as the blade makes contact, sinking into flesh, into bone. Then a gurgling sound. Then . . . nothing.

"Is everyone okay?" you shout, resuming a fighting stance, eyes still firmly shut. Then, a sharp talon grabs you by the throat, cutting off your air, lifting you off the floor.

"Slayer of the vampires," it says, its voice low and silky. "Your time on earth is over. Look upon my face, and know the hidden depths of your own despair."

Something about K'adolh's voice, commanding, seductive, makes you want to obey. Your eyelids flutter ever so slightly, your legs swinging freely beneath you as he lifts you higher, higher. . . .

And then your foot taps something, and you hear the sound of your leather boot hitting metal. The handle of your ax, embedded in the demon's side.

You lift your leg and bring it down hard, directly on the ax handle. K'adolh grunts and drops you, and as you fall, you make sure to land directly in front of him, grabbing the ax and wrenching it from his gut.

"Thanks for holding on to this for me," you say, lifting the ax behind your back. "But it really does look better on you."

You swing the blade and feel it slice cleanly through the bone. You hear his skull hit something soft as it falls, followed by the thunderous clap of his ancient bones as they come crashing down to earth for the last time.

There's a loud burst of electricity, and suddenly everything in the room seems to come alive at once: the overhead lights, the computer terminal, the fax machine and photocopier in Giles's office. Your eyes take a moment to adjust before you're able to take in the scene in its entirety.

Giles, clutching Jenny Calendar, huddled together in the mess of a smashed display case. Xander, still unconscious on the floor beside the long study table. Cordelia, standing up tentatively behind the circulation desk, apparently completely unscathed, looking more annoyed than anything else. And, beside the now-destroyed ritual space, the headless body of K'adolh, his desiccated rib cage bound together by rags and teeming with thick maggots.

"Xander!" Cordy says with surprising concern

before going to his side. Giles helps Jenny stand, and they brush themselves off.

"He should be fine," you say. "Actually, that was kind of my fault. But it was for the best," you qualify, miming him choking himself.

"Well done," Giles says, joining you over K'adolh's rapidly self-consuming corpse.

"Yeah, well, now I see why you told me to keep my eyes closed."

"It was his gaze. Once made flesh, his power was in his gaze. I saw the glow of his eyes in the dark, just before I felt myself wanting to . . ." He stops there, then says once again, softer now, "Well done."

"Um . . . Buffy?" You turn. Willow, in the center of the pentagram, is still tied to the chair, her eyes firmly shut. "I . . . think there's something in my lap."

You look from Willow to the lifeless head of K'adolh, the Suicide King, where it grimly rests on top of her knees.

"Will," you say, walking over to her with an unpreventable smile, "you probably want to keep those eyes closed."

SLAYER ACTION:
Turn to page 53.

Epilogue

"**O**h, yeah . . . Angel. Don't stop. Yes. Right there. Yeah. *There.* There!"

"You like that?"

"Oh, God, yes . . . Where did you learn to do it like that?"

"Well, I've been around awhile."

"But . . . I never could have imagined that it . . . could be so good."

"Yeah, well, you're dealing with a professional."

"You mean, you have a masseur's license or something?" You roll onto your side as Angel finishes working on a kink in your neck.

"Well . . . okay. No. I was just being cocky."

"No comment." After a few moments you sit up and stretch your arms over your head, basking in the sensation setting your skin aglow, making you feel alive again, in a way only Angel can.

"So, how does it feel to save the world?"

"You mean again?"

He chuckles. "Now who's being cocky?"

"It feels wonderful," you say, reaching up to caress his cheek. "Everyone seems to be doing well. Xander's nursing a mild concussion, Willow's powering her way back from the brink of demon-induced suicidal thoughts, Giles and Jenny are going away for the weekend to better nurse their cuts and bruises, and Cordelia's . . . Cordelia."

"Nice to know some things never change, isn't it?"

"It's really crazy," you say. "I mean, here we all are, depressed, questioning the meaning of life, why we're here, why we have to go through these stupid routines that make up our everyday lives, lost, doubting, unable to connect, alone, afraid. . . . I just realized that as bad as things get, we can kill those demons. We can change the way we see the world, the way we treat ourselves. We can make things better, move out of the darkness into the light. . . ." He gives you a sideways glance. "Move into the light metaphorically speaking," you add.

"You really believe that?" he asks. Something about his face in the moonlight streaming through his open window makes you want to hold him forever.

"I really believe that," you reply honestly.

"I don't know if . . . I don't know if you can slay all your demons. Some of them you've earned. You can spend five, ten, a hundred lifetimes, and they'll always be there." His eyes, filled with such sadness, pierce you to the core.

"Kill one demon at a time, Angel," you say, leaning in for a kiss. "Just one demon at a time."

THE END

Night begins to fall as you and the gals walk out of the Sun Cinema movie theater. "Well, that was a real pick-me-up," Cordelia sneers, rolling her eyes. "Depressing much? By the end I felt like sticking *my* head in the oven. To think you've passed on a lighthearted appointment with the grief counselor for that suicide fest. Paging Dr. Irony."

"I know what you mean," you say. "It kind of creeped me out, though, given what's been going on at school. Maybe we should have read the reviews."

"But wasn't it sort of romantic?" Willow says, her eyes widening with wonder. "Gwyneth and the other poet loved each other so much, but it just wasn't enough, no matter what they did." Angel's face passes through your mind's eye, but you purposefully blink it away.

"You guys want to grab a latte?" Cordy suggests, gesturing down the street in the direction of the Espresso Pump.

"I really should get going," you reply. "I have a ton of work to do, massive art project included."

"Okay, but don't forget, Devon's band is playing at the Bronze tonight, and I expect to see you there. I'll be the one standing at the side of the stage looking hot and bored." You say good-bye to Willow and Cordy and head down the block, only to see Xander running toward you, flapping his arms with excitement.

"Code red! Code red!" he practically shouts, gesticulating wildly.

"Is that supposed to mean something to me?" you ask. "Because if it does, I must have cut that class."

"Code reds are for suspicious deaths," he replies matter-of-factly.

"And what does that make code blues?"

"Suspicious . . . slide guitar players. Anyway, we may have a situation. Mr. Teal—the grief counselor they brought in—he was found about an hour ago hanging from the ceiling in Snyder's office."

"Hanging from the ceiling in a batty kind of way?"

"Well, sure, if the bat's dead and swinging from the ceiling fan by his necktie."

"He hung himself?" you blurt out, stunned. Silence. "Sorry. He *hanged* himself?"

"Either way, all signs point to yes. It looks like he took a short walk off a shorter chair."

A suicide counselor killing himself, at a high school, in the middle of the day no less? Code red indeed. "Oh well. So much for my art project. I better book back to school for a little recon and find out what's afoot."

"Not sure that's such a good idea, Bufferino. As I was heading home I saw the entire Sunnydale police force pass by with sirens ablazing. Either there's a Mr. Donut giveaway on the other side of town, or they were on their way over to the school."

"Did you hear anything else?"

"Just one thing. I happened to catch Snyder talking to his assistant as they were heading down the hall past my locker. Said something about accommodations, and 'vestment lands' or 'vast moor lands.'"

"Could it have been the Westmoreland House?"

"That sounds right. Mean anything to you?"

"Yeah," you reply. "It's a cute little bed-and-breakfast place near school. My dad was going to stay there a couple of months ago before he ditched to go to Hawaii with his new scag instead."

"Maybe that's where Mr. Teal's been staying."

"Could be. There might be something for me to check out there."

SLAYER CHOICE:

Do you decide to . . .

❧ head back to school to investigate the potential scene of the crime? *If yes, turn to page 59.*

❧ go instead to the B&B where the grief counselor was possibly staying while in town? *If yes, turn to page 66.*

You creep down the hallway outside Principal Snyder's office, careful not to alert anyone to your presence on school grounds after hours. It was difficult enough making it safely inside the building; with a dozen police and emergency vehicles parked outside, Sunnydale High looks more like the scene of a siege than that of one man's suicide. Edging toward the open doorway, you keep close to the wall, straining to hear the voices inside.

"So what you're telling me is, one of the students simply found him swinging here?" you hear a man inside say, his voice a little familiar.

"That's right, sir. We've cordoned off the campus and taken the names of everyone in and around this part of the building. The police have told us they're conducting interviews with any potential witnesses, anyone who may have seen Mr. Teal before his death, or any suspicious activity." That's Snyder talking. *Who's he calling "sir"?* you think to yourself.

"Gee whiz. Suspicious activity in our sleepy little burg? Imagine that." You crouch down for a closer look, but your view into the office is partially obstructed by the half-open door. "Did word get out about what happened here?"

"I'm afraid so. By tomorrow morning the whole town will know about this."

"That's a real shame. Not good news. Not good news at all. He sure does look peaceful, though. Except for his tongue lolling out like that. Hand me that chair, would you? There. That's better. Now there's a portrait Norman Rockwell forgot to paint. Takes your breath away, doesn't it?"

"Um, yes, Mr. Mayor, if you say so." *What's the Mayor doing here?* "Why he chose to end his life this way, however, inside my school, I cannot even begin to comprehend."

"Oh, don't be so hard on the poor man. He didn't choose this for himself. Quite the contrary."

"What do you mean? He hanged himself."

"He sure did. But it wasn't a suicide."

"What are you talking about?" you hear Snyder say, his bewilderment raising his voice an octave.

"Oh, when you've been around the block as long as I have, my good man, you learn to pick up on the signs."

"Do you think this is linked to the other four student suicides?" *Four? Isn't it supposed to be three?*

"You betcha. It seems as if we have an unwelcome visitor in town. A pesky one too."

"Excuse me, miss." Someone puts a hand on your shoulder and you turn, practically jumping out of your skin. "May I ask what it is you're doing?" Two men in decent suits and sunglasses are standing in front of you, blocking any means of escape; they look somewhat akin to Secret Service agents, and damned if you know how they got the drop on you. You spy one of their laminated badges: SECURITY, THE OFFICE OF MAYOR WILKINS. Suddenly the office door flies open and Snyder appears, quickly shutting it behind him.

"Young lady, you are in big, big trouble."

"I was just—coming back for a book I forgot in my locker," you stammer.

"Turn Miss Summers over to the police," Snyder says to the two goons.

"What are you talking about? I haven't done anything wrong."

"We've ascertained that the last completed appointment with Mr. Teal was with Jonathan Levenson, who confirmed the counselor was then alive and well. According to Mr. Teal's appointment sheet, you had the next scheduled meeting. Care to tell us what happened during that time?"

Oops. "I actually missed my appointment. I was with friends. I have an alibi. Many alibis. I mean, one alibi, but with lots of accomplices. I mean—"

"Tell it to the judge, Miss Summers. Gentlemen . . ."

SLAYER ACTION:
Turn to page 62.

You spend the next two hours at the police station sitting in a steel chair beside the detective's desk, answering question after question, defending your actions, your record ("Sure, yeah, I burned my school gym when I lived in L.A. Fine. But you really had to be there . . .") and pleading with them that you've done nothing wrong. But then they tell you the four words you've secretly been dreading since you arrived: "We've called your mother."

A few minutes later Joyce flies into the station, her hair a mess of tight tangles framing her face. She looks like she's been hit by a truck. No, two trucks. You turn away from her and look down at the concrete floor, a wash of undeserved shame flushing your face.

"Oh, Buffy." You look up at her again and your heart breaks.

"Mom, before you say anything, I need you to know I didn't do anything wrong. You have to believe me. I know I'm not perfect, and some things in my life haven't gone quite as well as I've hoped, but I do not deserve to be here."

"I know, sweetheart, I know. I couldn't agree with you more." Joyce kneels down beside you and puts her hands on yours, holding them tight. "It was a mistake for us to come here. I realize that now. It's my fault, and you deserve an apology."

"What . . . what are you talking about?"

"I just got off the phone with your father. We've decided that it would be best for you to go live with him for a few months."

"Are you *serious*?" you nearly scream, yanking

your hands from hers as you would from a pot of scalding water. "Have you lost it?"

"School just isn't the right environment for you, Buffy. Not now. We think a break would do you some good. You could get some counseling, try to work through whatever demons seem to be constantly plaguing you. Especially with all of these student suicides going on . . . I'm just not comfortable with you here in Sunnydale anymore."

"But you can't do this," you insist, beginning to feel light-headed, a strange sense of unreality taking over. "You can't send me away from here. I need to be here. I need to fight . . ." *How to explain? How?*

"I'm sorry, honey. The decision's already been made. Your father's coming to pick you up first thing tomorrow morning."

"Mom, you can't send me to live with him!" you shout, changing tack, trying to appeal to her severe dislike of your father. "He travels all the time. I'll be unsupervised! I'll run amok! And he's a bad role model. He's a philanderer, and a cheater, and . . ."

Your mother fixes you with a stony glare, and you know there's no more to say; you have nothing left. You look from her to the detective behind the desk, who is doing a poor job of pretending not to listen to your argument, and then back to your mother. Your knees are weak and shaking with righteous anger. You swallow once and stand, momentarily defeated.

"I'll go pack my things."

THE END

The Sunnydale docks, once used as a navy yard but now a run-down port of call for importers, exporters, and lowlifes, seem unusually foreboding tonight. Even the small amount of light shining from the streetlamps high overhead doesn't seem to penetrate the thick foggy air all the way down to the ground. You're not exactly sure whom you're looking for either. Every wandering junkie and prostitute looking for business seems a potential demon until you get close enough to stare into their sad, all-too-human eyes and mutter a quiet, "Sorry, I thought you were someone else." Then you hurry off in your search for the clan of Miquot demons.

After an hour or so you happen upon Pier 7, which is attached to an old abandoned warehouse that reeks of demon life. You slip silently inside through a rusty open door and head down a steep set of stairs to a catwalk stretching over the vast dark space of the warehouse floor below.

Suddenly there is a low growl coming from the other side of the walkway, followed by footfall. You crouch into a battle stance, but then the unexpected happens. A powerful brightness pierces the warehouse, and you're blinded; a large set of floodlights on the ceiling has been illuminated, all pointed directly at you.

With a large heaving sound of metal on metal, you feel the world spin out from beneath you as the catwalk is wrenched from its moorings on either side, sliding you off and sending you spinning to the floor below. You land flat on your back and the wind is knocked out of you, your strength along with it. And then, with horror, you watch in the bright light as the catwalk comes crashing down on top of you in a gruesome mess of chains and bent metal.

The pain you feel is excruciating, followed by very little pain at all; trapped beneath the twisted remains of the catwalk, you can no longer feel your extremities, or very much of anything except panic and fear. In your limited line of vision, you see a shadow fall over you, followed by another, and another, as the Miquot clan gathers around you to admire its prey.

"Slayer," one of them grunts. "We've been expecting you."

It's then that you realize you've been set up, and your fear is now colored with anger. Even before a retractable blade appears from beneath the arm of one of the demons, you know you're not going to get out of this one alive.

THE END

You walk up a wide path laid with bricks to the Westmoreland House Bed-and-Breakfast, which is situated among a grove of apple trees currently bearing their fruit. The bright red globes dotting the branches remind you of Christmas decorations; though the holiday is still two months away, you're already dreading it. Since your parents' divorce, every forced effort at yuletide cheer either you or your mother makes seems to land with a resounding thud. *Maybe this year will be different,* you think. *Maybe Dad will come to town for a few days, take me ice-skating, spend some real time with us. . . .* But no. That's just wishful thinking. You and your mom will most likely be alone again, you up on the stepladder, taking the angel from her hand to hang on the top of the tree. Just like last year.

You open the screen door and step inside. "Hello?" you call out, but there's no response, so you walk over to the small makeshift reception area. On top of the counter is a reservation book, open to today, and under the column marked "Room Three" you find the name "Teal" written in red ink. Making your way up the stairs, you cross the second-floor landing and go to the third door on the left, which is closed. You knock and wait a few moments before opening the door and slipping in, closing it quietly behind you.

The curtains on the window are drawn, the room dark. You feel your way along the wall and reach into the closet, turning the bulb on by its cord so that only a small amount of light seeps into the room, illuminating it just enough for you to make out your surroundings.

Beside the neatly made bed covered with a homey quilt is a small stand, atop which is a large black suitcase, the kind with wheels on the bottom. You open it and reach in, feeling around inside. Nothing seems of particular import: some clothes, a toiletry bag, a pair of men's brown leather shoes. You run your hand along the bottom of the suitcase, which is when you feel an unusual lump beneath the canvas.

You carefully take the contents out of the top of the suitcase, then place it on the bed, searching the inside lining for a zipper or catch, which is difficult in the near darkness. Then you find a small latch. After a few moments of fiddling, it snaps open, and you're able to lift out the false bottom to see what's inside.

Reaching in, you pull out an object about the size of a milk carton and wrapped in a cloth of dark red velvet. You slip it out of its protective sleeve and see that it's a smallish wooden box, emblazoned with the image of a crescent moon. You lift the box up to your ear and shake it a little, reminded once more of Christmas and the challenge of trying to guess what your brightly wrapped gifts contain the night before. As is the case on Christmas Eve, you find yourself too impatient to wait any longer, and begin trying to open the box.

Just then you hear the unmistakable sound of a floorboard creaking on the landing outside the door. With no time to return the contents of the suitcase to their rightful place, you dive toward the closet, box in hand, and turn off the light, shutting yourself inside. A moment later the door to the room opens and the light switch flicks on.

"Where is it?" you hear a man's voice say as he moves into the room.

"In the bottom of the suitcase," a woman replies. You hear the door shut behind them.

"I don't . . . I don't see it."

"Someone's been here. Someone's taken the box!"

"Are you sure? Perhaps Tealius has hidden it someplace. Or perhaps Ibrahim is holding it someplace safe."

"No. The map is gone. It's fallen into the hands of the Serpentines."

"Then all is lost, Anna. Unless . . ."

Silence. A long, cold, heavy silence. You've never been much of a fan of it, but it's never sounded quite so deadly before. Especially once it's broken by the sound of the closet door slowly sliding open . . .

You cannonball out of the closet, knocking down the man dressed in white in front of you before rolling and leaping up onto the bed. Jumping up, you use the wooden box in your hand to smash the light fixture overhead, plunging the room back into total darkness.

"Ohr chadash!" the woman intones, and a burst of light explodes from her hands, illuminating the room once more. *No fair,* you think, ducking down behind the bed. You reach up, yank the quilt off the bed, and leap forward, throwing the quilt over the silver-haired woman, and then tackle her with the force of ten linebackers. Just before you hit the floor, you can sense how delicate she is in your arms, and you put a hand down in front of you to keep from doing her any grievous harm.

Now's your chance to take the box and run; surely Giles can figure out its significance. Then again, this might be your only chance to find out who these jokers are and what it is they want. The man is out cold, but the woman still appears conscious, albeit incapacitated, wrapped up in the quilt beneath you. You didn't like the little lightshow she pulled, however, and don't know what other tricks they may have up their sleeves. Decisions, decisions—what's a slayer to do?

SLAYER CHOICE:

Do you decide to . . .

❘ take the wooden box to Giles? *If yes, turn to page 120.*

❘ spend a little face time with your new friends? *If yes, turn to page 70.*

Start at the beginning," you say, leaning over the woman, who you can now see is well into her fifties, far older than you originally suspected. "Tell me who you are, what you're doing here, your mission, habits, hobbies, everything. Leave anything out, and my face will be the last you ever see."

"I'll tell you nothing, Serpentine!" the woman seethes. "I'm prepared to die, so your threats scare me not."

"Die? Who said I was going to kill you?" You take out a stake from where you keep it in your jacket pocket, bringing the point down directly above her left eye. "All I said was that my face would be the last you ever see."

"You kill vampires?" she says, the bravado draining out of her voice.

"Uh, yeah, I'm kinda in charge of that."

"You're the Slayer," she says, her face alight with recognition.

"The one, the only."

"In this generation, at least," she scoffs. "There have been others before you, as there have been others before myself."

"No need to get all technical on me, lady. Way to bring a girl down. Yeesh."

"I befriended a slayer once," she says, surprising you. "You're tools of death. Cogs in the twilight machinery of good versus evil. Surely a useless battle, one that can never be properly won through violence."

"Again with the flattery. You're going to make me blush. Now, in case you forgot, we're in the middle of an interrogation. So start talking."

"We are members of the Order of Shifrah," she begins hesitantly, "the sworn enemies of the Serpentine One who feeds off the dark corners of the mind and brings self-death to those in his path."

"The Serpentine One? Is that supposed to mean something to me?"

"He is known by many names. He of the Forked Tongue, the Cunning One, the Suicide King. But he was first called K'adolh, the Nightwalker."

"Doesn't sound so bad. What's your beef?"

"Our order was the first to encounter K'adolh, when our ancestors were enslaved in ancient Egypt. We were able to contain him by trapping him within a scroll of papyrus. Unfortunately, before we could properly study him, the scroll was stolen from us. Though the demon king remains incorporeal, he is still able to utilize a fraction of his vast power to move from host to host, instilling midnight thoughts in his victims and feeding off the resulting despair."

You watch her face, and for just a quick moment, her eyes dart away, in the direction of the wooden box at your side. "What's with the box?" you ask.

"It . . . *contains* the Shifran map, the only means by which we are able to track K'adolh on his murderous path throughout the ages. It belongs to us."

"Right now it belongs to me. And I've been looking for something spiffy to keep my jewelry in, so that works out nicely. What's the story with Mr. Teal, the grief counselor?"

"He is . . . *was* Tealius, our partner, who has been following the trail of blood for years. He is no longer of this plane. He has fallen to the Serpentine One."

"We will all fall to the Dark One, should you fail to return the box," the man on the floor in front of the closet says, conscious now and rubbing the back of his head. "We must use it to find him, and kill him."

"And how do you plan on doing that?" you ask, watching him carefully.

"We will destroy his current host, before he is able to switch vessels."

"I don't get it. Don't all his victims kill themselves anyway?"

"Yes," the woman replies, "but not before K'adolh leaves them, which he is able to do through contact with any form of paper. There was a flaw in the initial binding ritual. Our people have been tracking him ever since."

"Well, I hate to be a party pooper, but whether they're hosting a suicide demon or not, I don't let human beings get killed on my watch. I'm funny that way."

"Then return the map you've stolen from us, and we'll be on our way."

Just then you hear a loud crash coming from somewhere below. The man rises with surprising speed and goes to the window, pulling back the curtain. "They're here," he says ominously.

"Who's here?" you ask. "I thought He of the Paper Products was incorporeal."

"His followers," the man replies, going flat against the wall. "The Cult of K'adolh. They've come for the map."

"We haven't much time," the woman says. You can see the panic in her eyes in the dim glow of light still emanating from somewhere inside her. "Return the box to us, and we'll be able to protect you. Otherwise . . ."

Now you can hear footsteps on the stairs, moving fast. You look from her to the man, and back at the box in your hand. How much can you trust these two?

SLAYER CHOICE:

Do you decide to . . .

❚ hold on to the box and take your chances with this supposed Cult of K'adolh? *If yes, turn to page 123.*

❚ hand over the box and hope they're sincere about their offer of protection? *If yes, turn to page 74.*

"Okay," you say, standing and unraveling the woman from the quilt before handing her the box. "But keep in mind, I don't take kindly to being backstabbed. Frontstabbing, too, for the record." The woman stands and takes the box, her other hand going to her mouth, index finger raised.

"Shhh . . . ," she says in a soft whisper. Then, a single word: *"Sanveyr."*

The door flies open, and you hold your breath as three figures dressed in hooded robes storm into the room. Nothing appears to have changed, not you, not the man and woman beside you, nor the glowing light emanating from her; nevertheless, the men walk right past you to the emptied suitcase on the bed.

"It's gone!" one of them cries, hurling the suitcase against the wall.

"The order has already retrieved it."

"What now?"

"We continue the hunt for the current vessel without the map. K'adolh will come to us this night; it is predestined."

You watch them walk past you; on top of their sleek cowls are stitched narrow golden eyes, as if to replicate those of a snake, staring at you eerily out of the darkness. A shiver runs down your spine as you continue to hold your breath while they leave the room and head back downstairs and out of the bed-and-breakfast.

"Let me guess: the Serpentines?" you whisper.

"Yes," the woman says, holding the box close to

her chest. "They'll stop at nothing to return their king to his original form."

"We must hurry," the man says, "before they decide to double back. Will you be safe making your way home?"

"Honestly, I'm more concerned about whether or not you'll be safe, even with that handy-dandy invisibility spell, if that's what that was. Really cool, by the way."

"Thank you," the woman said, a barely perceptible smile briefly passing over her lips. "We've just arrived in your town, upon our realization that Tealius—or Douglas Teal, as he was known to you—had been killed by the Suicide King. Might you have a suggestion where we could stay? I don't imagine spending another night in this inn would be the wisest idea. Do you know of somewhere, a safe house of some kind, perhaps?"

You have a sudden image of the two of them asleep on your bedroom floor, and your mother walking in to wake you up in the morning; for some things there are simply no adequate explanations. You look at them, then out the window, and back. "I think I can come up with something."

"Buffy, I hope you know what you're doing," Giles says, nervously wiping his glasses with a handkerchief. "I'm not in the habit of taking in strangers, especially under these circumstances."

"Why not?" Cordelia asks, throwing her hands up.

"It's not like they're out to steal your expensive . . ." She casts her discerning gaze over the contents of Giles's apartment, her voice trailing off. She quietly drops down onto the couch, crossing her legs.

"Thank you, Cordelia. I can feel the approximate sensation of reassurance washing over me."

"It's just until we can find out where this demon guy is," you say, "and how to stop him."

"According to what you heard the people who broke into the bed-and-breakfast—that is, the people who broke in after you did, and who are after these supposed members of the Order of Shifrah—say, it was prophesied K'adolh would return to them tonight. If their information is accurate, that doesn't leave us much time."

"Well, let's get started then." The doorbell rings, and the Shifrans jump up nervously from where they've been sitting cross-legged on the floor in the middle of the living room. You open the door, and Willow and Xander hobble in, a stack of books in each of their arms.

"Did someone order the entire demon possession and prophesy section of the library?" Xander asks, slamming his stack down on the coffee table. He turns to the man and woman, both dressed in white. "Greetings, members of a mysterious mystical sect."

"Xander, Willow, this is Anna and Ilon. We'll be helping them put a stop to this demon, once and for all."

"Sounds like a plan to me," Willow says. "Or, at least, you know, a concept, or a proposal! A fine proposal. But . . . what exactly *is* the plan again?"

"We're going to use the order's map—that's what's inside that box there—to locate K'adolh by locating his current host, whomever it is he went into after he left the grief counselor's body. Once we find that person, we're going to contain them, and prevent them from doing any harm to themselves while we figure out a way to extract the demon from the host."

"I . . . I don't think that's going to be possible," Anna says. "It's our mission to end the misery K'adolh has brought into this realm by any means necessary. The host must be expendable."

"I thought we went over this already," you say, exasperated. "No one dies, understand? There's got to be another way. Guys, let's get cracking on the research tip. There must be something in one of these books about how we can safely remove K'adolh from his victim."

"There may be one way," Ilon says, looking to Anna and then back at you. "If we can capture the scroll."

"Capture the scroll? I love that game!" Xander says. You glare at him and he sheepishly lowers himself onto the couch next to Cordy.

"What scroll? The one your people used to trap K'adolh in the first place?"

"Yes," Anna replies. "It's been lost to us for millennia, of course, but it must be nearby if the Cult of K'adolh is planning to recorporealize their master. Perhaps we can use it to trap him once more."

It makes sense, but suddenly you're not so sure. How well do you know Anna and Ilon anyway? Do

you really want to leave them alone with your friends?
On the other hand, if attaining the scroll is the only
way to prevent any further loss of life, can you afford
to take that chance, especially when the Cult of
K'adolh may be using it at any moment to give new
life to their demon king?

SLAYER CHOICE:

Do you decide to . . .

\ leave the gang and go find the scroll? *If yes, turn
to page 79.*

\ stick around and make sure the Order of Shifrah
is all that they seem? *If yes, turn to page 128.*

"Great. I'm on scroll patrol then." You lift your leather jacket off the back of a chair and slip it on. "You guys use the map to find us our demon, and in the meantime I'll go find the scroll."

"Buffy," Giles says, grabbing you by the arm just before you head out the door, practically dragging you into the kitchen. "I don't think you're acting with very much forethought. We don't know enough yet about these people—the Order of Shifrah, the Cult of K'adolh. We can't take what they say at face value. While you're out collecting artifacts for them, who knows what their true intentions are?"

"What other choice do I have? Sit around and wait for K'adolh to kill his next victim? Or worse, wait until his followers use the scroll to rebirth him or whatever and have him kill us all? If you have any other suggestions, I'm all ears."

"Just . . . be careful," Giles says, sighing with resignation.

"I always try." He looks so defeated you feel like kissing him good-bye on the cheek, but then, horrified at the thought, you back slowly away and out the door.

Where to start? You can head over to the demon hangouts, specifically Willy's bar, shake him down for any news he may have about a new power in town. Then there's always the Sunnydale Natural History Museum, artifact central. Maybe there's some information to be gleaned there. Since the scroll seems to already be in the hands of the cult, however, your best bet is to find out where they're lurking and confront them directly. Sounds messy, but doable.

Halfway down the block you stop walking, and an idea enters your head. If anyone in this town knows where to find a creepy artifact, the possession of which could either bring about hell on earth or go for a mighty steep price to the highest bidder, who would that be? *Of course.* You smile, and begin to hurry your pace.

"La doo dum dee, ya dum dee doo. La doo dum me, ya dum dee you. La doo dum—"

"Dru, would you knock it off already?"

"I can hear him singing in my head. La doo dum dee, ya dum dee doo."

"That's how we knew about him, isn't it? But we don't *all* have to hear him singing in our heads, love. Keep it down at least."

Seriously, you think. Drusilla's been crooning away since you crept into her and Spike's factory lair fifteen minutes ago; it's all you can do to keep from leaping out from your hiding place behind a large shipping crate and cramming a stake down her throat. At least she seems distracted. She's brittle and sickly, but you're still unsure of the depths of Drusilla's powers, and you're willing to put up with anything that keeps her unaware of your presence.

"But he makes such beautiful music," she trills, spinning across the room as she claps her hands above her head to some rhythm only she can hear. "Let's make music with him, Spike, pretty please? I do love to listen to the little kittens mew as they scratch at their own skins."

"There'll be plenty of that going on come tomorrow," Spike says, standing. He's hunched over something on the table in front of him, something large, but from where you're crouching you can't get a glimpse of what it may be. "First things first."

"First things are always first," Dru grumbles, pouting. "I want last things first for once. It's only fair and they never get their turn."

"There's a time for everything," he says, going to her, taking her in his arms. A queer shiver runs down your spine. "And we've made a promise. You don't want to upset the nice demon cult, now, do you?" She shakes her head like a petulant child. "That's my pet. That's my sweet pet."

They begin to kiss passionately, as if they're attempting to consume each other, which, for the creatures of the night that they are, shouldn't strike you as particularly disturbing. But somehow it does. To think that Angel was once part of their little gang turns your stomach, but you shake the thought away, peering out from behind the crate to take a gander at what's on the table.

Tied to the tabletop in what appear to be thick coils of copper wire is an extremely tall boy about your age, a piece of duct tape covering his mouth. He is completely motionless, save his eyes, which are darting back and forth, wild with fear. This was not part of the plan.

"Mr. Spike," Drusilla purrs, tilting back from Spike's embrace, "I'm *so* very hungry."

"Now, now, there's food on the way. And this one, he doesn't belong to us."

"But he's so scared. The fear, it seasons them to perfection."

"Listen to me," he says, grabbing her forcefully; a

shudder of delight passes over her face. "He's not ours. They're coming to take him away, and we're getting our payment, fair and square. A deal's a deal."

"Humph," she exclaims, pulling away. "Spike is no fun. Won't give his pet a scrap of food, he won't." Drusilla lurches over to the other side of the table, putting her face uncomfortably close to that of the terrified boy. "How did you get in there?" she says, tapping the boy's forehead with a sharpened fingernail. "How did you get inside there, without making so much as a cut?" She pulls back and whirls around the room once more. "La doo dum dee, ya dum dee doo . . ."

Not only is this poor kid being held captive by two of the most bloodthirsty killers you've ever come across, but it sounds as if he's about to be handed over to a demon cult with even worse designs. How best to save him? Should you take on Spike and Dru, with him still tied to the table, defenseless, or wait until the cult arrives and follow them, hoping for a more opportune time to rescue him?

SLAYER CHOICE:

Do you decide to . . .

❙ fight Spike and Dru? *If yes, turn to page 131.*

❙ wait until the cult arrives, and try to free the boy later? *If yes, turn to page 83.*

"You're wary of taking on both Spike and Drusilla, even without the hostage situation; best to wait until he's out of their hands to try to rescue him. It's only a few short minutes before the three vampire sentries you evaded while sneaking into the lair enter, trailing eight or so figures, all dressed in dark brown hooded robes, the cowls adorned with golden snake eyes that flicker in the soft light of the vampires' cavernous haunt. *So many of them!* Your heart begins to race. Maybe you should have acted sooner after all.

"You got the goods?" Spike barks at the lead man.

"We've kept our promise." The cultists part in unison, and from behind the three vampire lackeys, four more hooded figures step forward, each with a firm grip on one of Spike and Dru's rewards. The blood drains from your face as Giles, Cordelia, Xander, and Willow are shoved into the center of the room, stumbling forward in front of where Spike is standing, arms crossed, a studied sneer curled across his lips.

"Kept your promise, have you?" he says, shaking his head. "I asked for the Slayer, you dimwits. Not her fan club."

"Is this not her?" one of the hooded figures, a young woman, says, gesturing at Willow, who stares defiantly back at her despite her obvious terror.

"Does she look like the Slayer to you? Or is that what she told you?" Spike reaches down and lifts Willow up by her favorite red shirt adorned with two laughing cartoon dogs. "You playing at being the Chosen One, Red?" he snarls, his features transforming into his true face, the grim visage of the undead. "I'd love to see you try and take me on." Xander jumps at Spike, who bats him away with an open hand, sending him sprawling underneath the table, the wind knocked out of him.

"Xander!" Cordy shouts, rushing to his side.

"It matters not," the lead cultist says. "The remainder of the Order of Shifrah is dead. The time for K'adolh to walk the earth once more is anon. We shall commence the necessary ritual. Here. Now."

"A deal's a deal, four eyes." Spike lets go of Willow, and she falls to the floor hard; you see Giles wince as if he felt the blow himself.

"Didn't your mother teach you, Spike?" Drusilla chides, moving her body back and forth in small circles. "Snakes don't keep their word. They speak from one fork of the tongue, and lick, lick, lick with the other."

"Thank you, Dru," Spike replies, barely containing his seething anger. "That's very helpful to me now."

Suddenly an invisible force covers your mouth, and you are about to let out an involuntary yelp when a soft voice whispers inside your head. "Shhh . . . Don't move. It's Anna." Anticipating your rush of questions, she continues. "Ilon is dead, but I live . . . for a short time, at least. I'm here, beside you." *I have to do something,* you think. "I know," she replies in your mind. "And you shall do it in the name of the righteous. Unseen." You can hear her breathing next to you, and then, low but still audible, *"Sanveyr."*

"What was that?" Spike says, craning his neck to look behind the shipping crate where you're crouched. He's staring right at you, but somehow through you.

Let the fun begin, you think, rolling out from your hiding place and jumping up on the table beside the captive boy. Spike seems to sense you somehow, so he gets to go first. You leap into the air and spin, delivering a wicked roundhouse kick to his face, relishing the sound of his jaw cracking as a blood-soaked tooth pops out of his jaw, whistling across the room. Drusilla watches it hit the floor and begins to pivot, but not before you pull a stake out of your jacket pocket and chuck it at her. It plunges into her, just missing her heart by an inch or so, but she reels backward nevertheless, gasping with shock at the projectile lodged in her upper chest.

"Scatter!" one of the cult members shrieks, and they begin ducking for cover. One of them pulls out a short iron dagger and begins wildly slashing at the air; you go to him, punch him square in the face and pull the knife from his hand, tossing it across the room toward Giles, who plucks it from the air and begins trying to free the boy from the table. From behind you one of the Serpentines manages to find your shoulder and grab it, but you whip around, lifting him from the ground, and hurl him into one of his compatriots, flattening them both.

Just then you feel a wave of white-hot energy pass through you, and from the way Willow is suddenly staring at you, you realize the invisibility spell has evaporated. *Nice while it lasted,* you think, ducking as a Serpentine attempts to tackle you. *Hopefully Anna is still hanging in there.* You see her crouching beside the table, visible now, clutching her stomach in pain.

"Child," she says in your mind, her discomfort palpable to you, "you must retrieve the scroll. *There*." She points up toward the rafters, where you see a lone cultist climbing up a ladder to the ceiling. You run toward one of the Serpentines and use his body as a springboard to leap from his shoulders, grabbing one of the lower rungs of the ladder.

"Oh no, you don't." You reach up and snare his ankle, and he stops, reaching into his belt for his knife. What you see curled up alongside the leather sheath, however, interests you far more than a mere weapon: the coveted scroll, the key to trapping K'adolh once more.

You pull yourself up and latch yourself onto the Serpentine before he can draw his knife, and suddenly you feel him let go of the ladder. "Look out below!" you shout, and the two of you tumble from the rafters, you using your strength to turn, so that he breaks your fall on the floor below.

"Buffy!" Willow shouts, and you look up. Spike and Dru are beating a hasty retreat into the shadows near the rear of the building, but the remaining Serpentines are rallying, cornering Giles and the demon-possessed boy in the center of the room. You yank the scroll from the unconscious cultist's belt and hold it up in the air.

"Hey, snake guys," you say. "Scroll much? I thought you needed this thing for something."

You see their eyes go wide beneath their cowls, but what surprises you is the hostage, who yanks the knife from Giles's hand, the cultists pulling him behind them, protecting him. His eyes suddenly glow golden, the irises split by thin, serpentlike red reeds. *"Slayer,"* he says then in a malevolent, unearthly voice. *"Deliver the scroll to my followers or this vessel will be broken."* He raises the knife to his throat.

"Buffy," you hear Anna say once more in your head, her words uneven but still determined. "Destroy the scroll. Do it fast. Do it now."

SLAYER CH⊕ICE:

Do you decide to . . .

❙ hand the scroll over to the Cult of K'adolh? *If yes, turn to page 136.*

❙ do what Anna says and destroy it? *If yes, turn to page 138.*

❙ refuse both requests and continue to fight? *If yes, turn to page 88.*

Whether you hand the scroll over or destroy it, you don't see how either option is going to save the boy K'adolh is currently inhabiting; he's probably going to be torn apart during the recorporealization ritual, or be made to cut his own throat. You've never been much for following orders anyway. Best to do it the Buffy way.

"You want this scroll so badly? Fine. Take it." You toss it high into the air, and watch it disappear into the darkness of the rafters. As all eyes are pointing upward, you sprint across the length of the room, taking a split second to leapfrog over the wall of Serpentines and come crashing down on K'adolh's current host, throwing him to the floor. You punch him in the face just hard enough to knock him unconscious, the knife falling from his hand. Xander, Cordelia, and Giles head into the fray, joining the pile of cult members clamoring for the scroll as if for a fumbled ball, shirts vs. hooded robes in the big game. In the resulting chaos Willow slides along the floor to assist Anna, where she is crumpled in a ball, blood beginning to soak through her white cloak.

You watch the scroll pass hands three, four times, keeping your eye on the prize as you kick and punch your way through what's left of the Cult of K'adolh. The last remaining Serpentine standing grabs the scroll, and a look of almost serene satisfaction passes over his half-cloaked face, but only for a moment. He looks around him at the bodies of his partners littering the floor, and then from Giles to Xander to Cordelia, who have him surrounded. You stroll over to him and, defeated, he puts his hands out in front of him in a conciliatory gesture. As if that's going to stop you from socking him.

"Yoink," you say as you take the scroll from him. He lowers his head in deference, and a reasonably lightweight right hook sends him to the ground. "Willow," you say, turning. "How is she doing?"

"I think she's going to be okay," she replies, crouched over Anna. "But we need to take her to the hospital."

"First . . . the ritual," Anna manages to say. "I'll pull through. But we need to do it soon, before the boy reawakens and K'adolh is able to control him once more."

"Let's get out of here before Spike and Dru get their nerve back or any of these snaky guys wake up."

"To the library, then," Giles says, leaning down to help Willow pick Anna up off the floor. They each take an arm and gingerly move her toward the exit. On the way out you notice Xander smiling to himself.

"What's gotten you so happy?" you ask.

"There's nothing like a good Snake Whacking Day to lift a guy's spirits," he replies, rubbing his bruised knuckles.

"Next time I'll get you a stick with your name on it: Xander's Whacking Off Stick." Silence. "Maybe not."

SLAYER ACTION:
Turn to page 90.

Epilogue

It's a beautiful night, the moon a sparkling crescent, and all's well in Sunnydale, or at least as well as can be expected in this town. Only one vamp rises in the cemetery, which Angel gallantly disposes of while you perch on the edge of a mausoleum, admiring his physique as he brushes the dust off his pants. He looks up at you and smiles. Your heart wants to melt but you won't let it, and instead you shiver.

"Are you cold? You look cold," he says, rushing to your side with concern. "Here, take my jacket," he blurts out nervously, removing it.

"You have to stop giving me your jackets. I have, like, five of them. Keep it."

"But you're shivering."

"It wasn't an 'I'm cold' shiver, it was . . . the other kind of shiver."

"Fear?" he asks, his eyes narrowing.

"No, a good kind of shiver. A happy shiver." He stands there for a few moments, hand extended, the leather jacket draped across his bare arm. "Fine," you say, rolling your eyes. "I'll take it. But if you keep behaving like such a gentleman, my mother's going to start wondering what I'm doing with all these large men's clothes in my closet." You slip it on and feel the cool leather against your skin and smile briefly. "It's funny," you say, staring up at the moon.

"What's that?"

"Since we trapped K'adolh in that scroll and destroyed it, everything's been pretty peachy. Except for what happened to that kid he infested, that is. He's going through some hard stuff—intensive counseling, nightmares, round-the-clock supervision . . . I just wonder sometimes. It seems like when we have something like a demon to blame for our problems, it makes everything pretty cut-and-dried. But when we don't have that excuse, when all we're battling is our own personal issues, it makes it much more scary, don't you think? I mean, can you imagine what it must feel like, how horrible it must be to wake up every morning and want to kill yourself?"

"Yes, I can," he says, staring you directly in the eye. "I know exactly how that feels. Except for the waking up in the morning part, that is." He breaks his stare and walks a step or two away before looking up at that stunning crescent moon. "Ever since that Romany curse gave me back my soul, I've had to live with the knowledge of what I did to all those innocent people, the pleasure I took in the agony they experienced in their last moments on earth. I can't tell you how many times I've thought about ending it all. But I'm different from some suicidal kid who's feeling lost and scared and alone. Me, I deserve that torment. I deserve the pain."

"No, you don't," you say emphatically, jumping down from your perch atop the mausoleum. "You're a good person, with a good heart. In fact, you're one of the best people I know."

"Am I really such a good person, Buffy?"

You go to him and put your arms around him. "Look at me," you say, and he lowers his gaze to meet yours, his eyes mournful and unsure. "You are living proof—or at least, undead proof—that, given a second chance, someone can make their life count. Every day you stand up for what's right and true and, yes, good. Not all curses are bad, Angel. You're not that monster anymore. You're a hero. You're my hero."

He smiles, taking your hands in his. "Thanks."

"Yeah, well, I mean it. And not just because of all the free jackets."

He puts his arm around you as the two of you begin to stroll toward the far side of the cemetery. There's still four more hours until the sun rises.

THE END

"**J**ust when you think you've seen it all . . ." Willow is curled up on the couch, a blanket around her, sipping hot chocolate from a large mug in the approximate shape of a duck. "I mean, I've seen dead bodies, wounded bodies, squidlike Hellmouth beasties, friends turned into vampires—"

"I know, Will. I know." You love her to death, you really do, but Willow's been going on like this for what must be an hour now. You can't help but feel that she shouldn't be quite so traumatized, which makes you feel guilty, but there it is. You've never seen her so upset, though, and all you can do is be there for her and listen.

"I just feel . . . I don't know . . . so sad inside. I feel terrible, Buffy. I don't know what's wrong with me."

"What you're feeling is perfectly normal. You're experiencing PVC symptoms, which any sane person would after walking in on that."

"Polyvinyl chloride?" Willow says, looking concerned.

"Oops. No, not that. I think I have some pants made out of that, though. I mean that other thing, where you have bad dreams and flashbacks and stuff."

"PTSD," she corrects you. "Oh, God, Buffy, am I going to start having nightmares? 'Cause I don't think I can handle those right now. We have a French test next week, and I haven't even started the pluperfect chapter yet and—"

"Willow, try to relax. Everything's going to be okay, I promise. Wigging out is not the answer."

"I'm not like you, Buffy," she says, staring into her

hot chocolate. "I'm not sure everything's going to turn out fine. I'm not strong. I'm scared."

"I get scared all the time. But you *are* strong. Believe me. I've seen you in action. You're going to power through this." You go to place a reassuring hand on her knee, but she flinches. "Sorry, I didn't mean to—"

"I'm just a little jumpy. I'll be fine," she says, nodding, but it's not entirely convincing.

The front door opens then and Sheila Rosenberg, Willow's mother, rushes in, dropping a tote bag crammed with books to the floor. "Oh, honey, are you all right? I came as fast as I could." She throws herself down on the couch between you and goes to hug her daughter. Willow lets out a shrill but largely stifled yelp before jumping up, her mug spilling all over the coffee table.

"She doesn't want to be touched," you say quietly.

"Of course, of course," Sheila says, putting her hands up. "You're suffering from posttraumatic stress, sweetheart. You'll probably experience some adverse reactions as a result—sleep disorders, inability to concentrate, anxiety. . . ." Willow bursts into tears and runs to her room, slamming the door behind her. "Did I say something wrong?" her mother asks you.

"She's still really upset." *In fact,* you think, *she seems to be doing even worse than when I first found her crying in the hallway outside the art studio.*

"Thanks for staying with her, Bunny. You're a good friend."

Bunny? "Yeah, uh, no problem. It's the least I can do."

"The school secretary called me at my office. She told me it was the grief counselor they had brought in because another student killed herself. What is going on in that place?"

"I don't know," you reply. *But I'm going to find out.* "If you don't mind, Mrs. Rosenberg, I'm going to get going. I'm sure my mom wants me home."

"I'm sure she does. Say hi for me, okay?"

"Will do."

As you make your way down Willow's block, you stop to think for a moment. Maybe you should just head home to your mother; she's probably heard the scuttlebutt and is worried sick about you. But that's not the way this Slayer gig works and—almost against your better judgment—you decide to go back to school for some snooping.

SLAYER ACTION:
Turn to page 59.

You grab the suicide note and dive out the window, clearing the sill just as Principal Snyder swings open the door to his office. "Good lord," you hear him exclaim, his tone not so very different from the one he uses to issue his usual stern warnings. "Get me the Mayor's office on the phone," he barks, most likely to his assistant cowering in the hallway.

Crawling a safe distance away from the open window, you stand and head toward the side of the building, where you sit on the edge of the courtyard fountain to peruse your stolen booty: the grief counselor's suicide note. You begin to read, and a chill slowly travels down your spine.

> *I'm the last person that should be doing this, but*
> *I find that I can no longer control my actions, nor*
> *these words that I am now writing. When I try*
> *Order must be*
> *Preserved*
> *Don't let*
> *Don't touch*
> *I'm so sorry to let you all down. I can't fight it*
> *anymore, and this is the only way I know how to*
> *stop it. Do not let it get to you, too.*

Okay . . . This isn't nearly as coherent as Diana Fitzgerald's suicide note, which Mr. Teal had read at the assembly, despite the beginning and ending lines, the latter of which eerily echo the words Diana herself used in her letter. Something about it is wigging you out, though you can't seem to put your finger on it. *Don't touch . . . Don't touch what?* You're seriously not a fan of the vague. Not to mention the strange way his hand seems steady in those beginning and ending bits, but in the middle the penmanship goes all sideways and spooky, as if the words were scrawled in the dark.

What to do now? You remember seeing the stack of suicide prevention pamphlets on Snyder's desk, with "Sunnydale Suicide Prevention Society (SSPS)" printed on them. Though you've never heard of it before, this group may be just the place to find out more about what's going on. You use one of the pay phones near the parking lot to get their address and phone number.

"Local information, please. Sunnydale Suicide Prevention Society."

"I'm sorry," the operator replies. "I'm not showing a listing for that name. Is everything all right? Are you having an emergency?"

"No, everything's fine. Thanks." You hang up the phone. *That's odd,* you think. *What kind of suicide prevention joint doesn't have a listed number?* You vaguely remember an address, over on President Street, from the back of the pamphlet and decide to head over there and see if you can find it on foot.

It doesn't take you long. In front of a gargantuan Victorian-style mansion with SUNNYDALE SUICIDE PREVENTION SOCIETY stenciled on a sign out front, at least ten cars are parked, along with a few bicycles strewn haphazardly across the lawn. You make your way up the narrow path of stones to the front of the building and step onto the porch; through the large front windows you can see inside, where forty or fifty people are milling about, seated in folding chairs or on the floor. You walk inside, and you can practically feel the heaviness in the air weighing you down. Everyone—kids, adults, even a few elderly folks—appears in a collective depressive daze, barely registering one another's presence. This is even worse than you could have imagined.

"Hello, dear," a mousy young woman in pearls says, approaching you. "Are you here to speak to a counselor?" She hands you a blue pamphlet with the word "Lonely?" on it, just like the one you saw among the grief counselor's possessions. "We'll get to you just as soon as we can. As you can see, we're having quite a busy day."

You take a newly vacated seat; a little while later a handsome man in his late twenties or early thirties sits down beside you and proceeds to bury his nose in a book. After a few minutes, thoroughly bored, you turn to him. "Reading anything good?"

"The Sorrows of Young Werther," he says in a slight and unfamiliar accent, showing you the cover of the book. "It's by Goethe."

"Sounds very . . . German."

"There's an interesting story behind the book, actually," he says, becoming quite animated. "It's about a man who kills himself following a doomed love affair. After it was published, it caused a sensation when it resulted in a number of copycat suicides."

"A little light reading to pass the time before your appointment?"

"Not exactly," he says, smiling. "More like 'know thine enemy as thyself.'"

"Forgive me for saying that you don't exactly seem like you're at the end of your rope."

"I could say the same about you, young lady."

"Well, okay, you got me," you reply, leaning in closer. "I'm just here doing research for a school project."

"I'm doing a bit of research myself," he says, extending his hand. "David Abraham of the *Mental Health Journal*."

"Buffy," you reply, smiling. You shake hands; as he pulls his back, you notice on his middle finger a signet ring with a crescent moon insignia identical to the one you spied among Mr. Teal's things. "Of the Sunnydale High School," you add.

"I've heard about what's happening at your school, all the . . . deaths," he says cryptically. "They've brought in a grief counselor, yes? How's that working out for you?"

"Not so well," you answer. "He's dead himself."

"What?" The man's face goes white. "Are you sure?" he whispers.

"I'm positive."

"He must have taken his ring off. He was always playing with that damn ring," he mumbles under his breath, then stops for a moment before asking, "How did he die?"

"He hanged himself. I saw the body."

"You found him?" he says, beginning to shake a little, dropping his book to the floor. Suddenly he looks like he fits right in here. "I must ask you something very important, and you must answer me truthfully," he says, his dark eyes staring you down. "Did you touch anything he may have handled before he died?"

You open your mouth, but you hedge, unsure of what to say, since of course you did touch a number of things at the scene, most conspicuously the suicide note now inside your jacket pocket. Who is this man, really? And why is he wearing the same ring that was found at the scene of the grief counselor's death? Before you can say anything, however, the woman who handed you the pamphlet reappears at the end of the hallway. "Buffy Summers," she calls. It's your turn.

"Don't go in there," the man beside you says. "You may be in grave danger. You must leave with me at once."

SLAYER CHOICE:

Do you decide to . . .

❚ trust this David Abraham guy and hightail it out of there with him? *If yes, turn to page 104.*

❚ proceed as planned and talk with the suicide-prevention folks? *If yes, turn to page 101.*

You allow the SSPS worker to show you down the long hallway, and she ushers you into a small and windowless room with a desk, a lamp, and, at the center, two folding chairs facing each other. "Have a seat, dear," she says. "I'll be with you in just a bit." After a minute or so you begin to relax a little. *See, there's nothing to worry about,* you say to yourself, sitting back in your chair. There's a poster print on the wall above the desk, and you find yourself staring at it. It's of a nude woman lying back, her eyes half closed, a snake coiled around her hand; someone is standing beside her, removing from her head an ornate crown. You recognize the work—maybe Mr. Blodgett showed a slide of it to your art class—as a depiction of Cleopatra, the Egyptian queen who killed herself by allowing a venomous snake to bite her.

Though beautifully rendered, it doesn't exactly strike you as the most appropriate image for a suicide prevention society. Maybe there *is* more going on here than you realize. In fact, your sense of ease is rapidly drifting south the longer you're kept waiting. What's it been now, five, ten minutes? It feels like you've been waiting an eternity. You're starting to feel anxious— hot, itchy, nauseous. You stand up, and that's when the dizziness hits you, so that, as you stumble against the wall, it's like walking through mud, each step an exercise in inertia. You try to open the door, but there's no handle, and it appears locked from the outside.

"Hello?" you shout, but there's no response. You pound on the door, but it feels as if it's made out of steel. You're beginning to panic now. *What is going on? What's happening to me?*

Suddenly the lights cut out, and it's then that you catch a strange, almost imperceptible sensation in the air. You realize with horror that something, perhaps a noxious gas or a paralyzing spell of some sort, is slowly taking you over. Fighting against it for as long as you can, you eventually crumble to the ground, trying to keep your mouth and nose covered while simultaneously gasping for breath. The room begins to hum, followed by a groaning sound of metal on metal, and you watch as the floor begins to open up on the other side of the room, revealing a dank cavern beneath. The desk slides off into the blackness, followed by the folding chairs, until, having nothing to hold on to for leverage, you fall, slipping into the abyss.

You come crashing down into what must be the basement of the building. Perhaps they meant for you to be out cold from the gas by now, but you're still lucid, barely. You're just awake enough to hear the sound of footfall all around you. From where you lie on the floor, you can just make out the hooded figures surrounding you, their amber, snakelike eyes glowing like fireflies in the dark.

"We welcome you," one of them says, leaning toward you. You can see now that the golden eyes are merely decorative, sewn onto his cowl. "We accept this sacrifice."

"Yeah, well, thanks for having me," you say, starting to fade from consciousness.

"All hail K'adolh," another intones.

"Hail K'adolh," the rest respond as one.

You want to fight, you really do, but you don't have an ounce of strength left in your body. Just before you black out, you see a pair of golden, serpentine eyes hovering above you, seemingly narrowing and coming closer, moving in for the kill.

THE END

You're halfway down the block before you halt and cross your arms, making it clear that you're not taking another step without some answers. "Look, I'm not going anywhere with you until you explain to me what's going on."

"Let's get off the main street," the man says. "It's not safe for us to talk out in the open."

You follow him into a nearby alleyway before he stops, waiting for you to catch up. Night has fallen all around you, a brisk wind creeping into the air. "Okay, Mr. Mysterious Guy, if that is your real name. Spill it. And if you're afraid I'm going to think you're crazy if you start talking about vampires or witchcraft or demon possession, let me put that thought out of your mind now. I want the truth."

"There is a great evil loose in this town," he begins, eyeing you suspiciously. "An evil that goes by many names. His true name is K'adolh. He is a demon that feeds off human misery and causes self-death, traveling from body to body, leaving destruction in his wake. I am a member of an ancient order that is charged with ending his time in this plane."

"How do you kill it?" you ask.

"We must obliterate whatever host he currently inhabits," he replies.

"So, you're planning on killing whatever innocent person he's possessing?"

"Precisely."

"That doesn't sound very orderly. Or fair. Or legal, even."

"I have worse news for you," he says matter-of-factly,

casually drawing a large serrated hunting knife from behind his back. "I suspect that person may be you."

"Did I neglect to mention the 'not fair' part?" you say as he slowly walks toward you.

"I'm very sorry," he replies, raising the knife. "My people have waited millennia for this moment."

"Yeah, well, I'm very sorry too then, because your peeps are going to have to wait a few more." You spin and deliver a roundhouse kick—into nothing. He's vanished. Gone. "Maybe we should go over that 'not fair' concept one more time." You take a deep breath and concentrate; he's got to be here somewhere. So you crouch into a battle stance, and listen, and wait. . . .

Suddenly you hear the sound of something whistling through the air just beside your right ear, and you turn, spinning to the side. You feel him brush past you, and extending your leg, you use his forward momentum to trip him. Once you hear him hit the ground, you throw yourself at the space where you imagine he landed, bringing your elbow down. You make contact, the familiar sensation of bone cracking against bone. You reach down and fumble to get your invisible assailant into a choke hold, the image of the nine-inch blade foremost in your mind. You pull him up by his neck and squeeze; the knife materializes out of thin air, clattering to the pavement at your feet.

"Okay, Casper, show yourself now, or you're going to be eating alley asphalt for dinner tonight." After a few more moments of resistance, he goes slack and rematerializes. You let go and give him a little shove for good measure, letting him stumble back against a brick wall. "Why don't you tell me what makes you think I'm the one doing the demon hosting."

"The Cunning One," he says, out of breath, his hands planted firmly on his knees. "Just before he . . . leads a victim to suicide . . . he leaves the body through the last piece of paper the host has touched. That's how he . . . escapes death himself."

"What makes you think that just because I'm the one who found him that I . . ." You reach into your jacket pocket, removing the grief counselor's suicide note. "Oh. Okay. Well, yeah, I took his suicide note. But that doesn't necessarily mean . . . It's possible that someone else . . . How can you be sure it's me?"

"I can't. Not without the Shifran map, which our order created to track K'adolh. It was in Tealius's possession. Now it could be in the hands of the Serpentines."

"Tealius?"

"The man you knew as Douglas Teal, the counselor brought to your school. He was a loyal member of the Order of Shifrah and has paid the ultimate sacrifice."

"And the Serpentines? Who are they?"

"The Cult of K'adolh, who seek to rebirth K'adolh into flesh form to walk this realm once more. They too have been searching for the current host. I have reason to believe they are the ones running the so-called suicide prevention society we just fled, in order to screen those individuals most likely to carry the virus that is K'adolh; they may be after us as we speak. Once they find you, you'll wish you'd let me kill you."

"Um, no, but thanks for your concern." You're beginning to feel a bit queasy; you're not sure if it's because there may actually be something wrong with you, or if it's merely the power of suggestion. "Surely there's another way to stop this thing without any more deaths."

"There may be one way . . . ," he says, then stops, his eyes going wide. You follow his gaze toward the entrance to the darkened alley, where you see half a dozen cloaked figures heading in your direction. "The Serpentines . . . they've found us," he gasps. He stands then, and, impossibly, the serrated knife is suddenly in his hand once more. "Run," he says. "I will hold them off as long as possible. You must recover the map. Go to it. Now!"

You're about to protest when, in a flash of light, you're blinded completely. Your eyes take a minute to adjust, and you find yourself no longer in the alleyway, but instead on the other side of town, in front of a familiar doorway in a familiar building. Once you've recovered your bearings, you step forward and swing open the door.

"Oh, hello, Buffy, I was just about to try to reach you." Giles, standing beside the entrance to his office, is busily stirring a cup of tea with a spoon and shuffles past you nonchalantly into the main room of the Sunnydale High library, where Angel, Cordelia, and Xander are sitting along one side of the study table. You feel as if you've stepped into some sort of dream.

Angel stands. "Buffy, are you okay? You were supposed to meet me at the cemetery an hour ago," he voices with concern.

"Oh, sorry . . . I've been having a really bad day."

"Well, I'm afraid it's not over yet," Giles says. "Angel confronted a group of strange fellows rushing through the graveyard; they were dressed in dark robes embroidered with some sort of snakelike designs. They were carrying this." He reaches toward the table and picks up a wooden box inscribed with a familiar crescent-moon insignia. "We've been trying to open it, to no avail. Whatever it is, it's no doubt of great import, and I can't seem to find any applicable information about it in my texts."

"Try under 'Shifrah, Order of,'" you say, plunking yourself down at the table. "There's a map inside, designed to locate the presence of a suicide-inducing demon named K'adolh." Cordelia and Xander stare at you, dumbfounded. "What? I'm only supposed to be the muscle around here? A girl can bust the knowledge now and then." Silence. "Okay, fine. I was mystically transported to your doorstep by one of these Shifrah people so I could recover the map. Happy now?" More silence. "And guys, let's work this fast, okay? We might not have much time. . . ."

SLAYER ACTION:
Turn to page 114.

"**A**re you sure you're ready for this?" Angel's face is only an inch or two from yours, so close you imagine that if he consumed oxygen you could feel his breath on your cheek.

"Does Molotov make a mean cocktail?" you reply, holding up one of the bottles.

"I don't know," he says, grinning slyly. "Let's find out." He takes a lighter out of his pocket and ignites the gasoline-soaked rag, and you stand, quickly releasing the makeshift explosive. It arcs over your hiding place behind a gravestone, and you watch the bottle sail through the air, taking a moment to appreciate its luminescent beauty against the dark sky before it crashes through the stained-glass window of the large mausoleum. Angel lights another and throws it, another window shattering, then the large popping sound inside, sending the structure up in flames.

It takes a few moments before the vampires begin to spill out of the entrance to the tomb, some already evaporating in fire and dust, and you ignite another bottle, pitching it at an unscathed vamp, who subsequently falls and dies, for the last time. Angel leaps out and runs after one whose pant leg is aflame, striking him to the ground before staking him. You see another one dart off between a row of graves, but you get a bead on it, lighting and throwing your last Molotov cocktail. It hits its mark and the creature goes down, howling, in a cloud of smoke. Soon it's all over, another vamp nest demolished. Score one more for the Chosen One.

"Wow . . . Would it be wrong to say that was kind

of fun?" you ask, brushing some graveyard dirt off your jeans.

"Oh, I don't know. It all depends on the company, I guess. Speaking of which . . ." Angel's head tilts up slightly, and he points with his chin toward the far end of the cemetery. "We may have missed a few." About a hundred yards from the burning mausoleum, barely visible in the dim night, you can see a few shadowy forms moving between the tombstones toward the cemetery gates. "Shall we?"

"Surely." You both take off running in slightly different paths, you in a fast and direct sprint toward your quarry, Angel in a roundabout route in the direction of the gates in order to cut off their means of egress. You use a grave marker as a launching pad, hurtling up into the air and coming down on two of the darkly clad figures, throwing them down. You reach for your stake and raise it as you roll the closest one onto his back, only to find two sets of eyes staring back at you: a pair of snakelike eyes embroidered on a long cowl, above two very frightened, very human ones, widening in fear.

"Angel!" you manage to get out before you're tackled by another one of them, who appears to be wielding some kind of ornate knife, the hilt of which is in the shape of a coiled snake.

"I know," he says, appearing beside you to deliver a blow with the heel of his hand to one of the hooded men's faces. You swing your leg forward, tripping the guy with the knife, and bring your elbow down hard on his solar plexus, knocking him out. There's one left standing, but not for long—Angel whips around, felling him with a high roundhouse kick.

You step over to the only conscious one, who's busy trying to stand, his feet catching on the bottom of his dark brown ceremonial robe. "Let me help you," you say, hauling him up by the back of his hood, the embroidered snake eyes sparkling in the dim moonlight. "Now, why don't you tell me what you nice folks are doing slithering around the cemetery?"

"I will tell you nothing," he says, shaking your hand off. "By morning all the world will know firsthand the power that is K'adolh."

"K'who now?"

"You cannot stop the Cult of K'adolh. You cannot stop our king." A glimmer of steel is all the warning you have; before you can act, the cloaked man raises a blade identical to that of his fallen confederate and swiftly plunges it into his chest. He falls to the ground and, following a chilling death rattle, is silent. A moment later you watch in grim fascination as his corpse slowly begins to shimmer, as if viewed through waves of noonday heat rising from a tar road. Seconds later his form is gone. You quickly turn, only to realize that the rest of the cult members have completely vanished as well.

"Uh, there *was* just a bunch of guys in weird snake outfits lying around here a second ago, right?"

"Yes," Angel replies. "Yes, there was."

"Whew. 'Cause for a second there—"

"Buffy, look." Angel takes a few steps and leans down beside one of the gravestones, returning with a smallish wooden box emblazoned with the image of a crescent moon. "Looks like they left us a present."

"Ooo! Gimme gimme gimme!"

"I don't think so," he says, wagging a finger in your direction. "Don't you remember what happened to Pandora?"

"Weren't they a metal band?"

"Very funny. Let's get this to Giles," he says, beginning to walk.

"Spoilsport. Hey," you say, staring at the design on the box, "I saw a ring with the same moon shape earlier. It was on top of Mr. Teal's things, the grief counselor who quote-unquote killed himself."

Angel stops. "A ring? That looked like this? A crescent moon insignia?"

"Yeah. Why?"

"Of course. It makes perfect sense. How could I be so . . . This must contain the Shifran map," he says, holding up the box. "It's the only known way to track the Suicide King."

"Okay. Explain, please."

"The Order of Shifrah is an ancient sect whose mission it is to track this demon that used to be called the Suicide King. He feeds off the misery of his victims before he exits their bodies and drives them to their deaths. I came across the Shifrans, I don't know, maybe a hundred and fifty years ago or so, when I was Angelus, in Dublin. They had this thing about not handling any paper touched by the person who committed suicide, something about a contagion. I don't really remember it that well."

"Whatever happened to, 'I'm constantly tormented by the perfect memory of all my horrible crimes,' et cetera and so forth?"

"I was drinking a lot at the time. Alcohol, I mean." He starts walking again, and you hurry to keep up. "We really better figure out what's going on here, Buffy. If the Suicide King's in town, and these followers of his are out there looking for him, it could mean a world of trouble for all of us."

SLAYER ACTION:
Turn to page 114.

The Order of Shifrah is a sect primarily associated with sorcery and mysticism, whose origins date back at least to the time of the pharaoh Amenhotep I in ancient Egypt,'" Giles begins, reading from one of his countless dusty old books stacked up on the library's study table. You, Cordelia, and Xander are seated across from him; you're waiting for Willow and Jenny Calendar to arrive to pitch in with the research, Angel having left to do some information gathering at a local demon haunt. "'The order, which first consisted of a small coven of witches enslaved by the pharaoh, was initially formed as a secret investigatory body to examine a disturbing epidemic: that of a suspected suicide contagion among the slaves.'"

"Because usually it's such a breeze being a slave to the pharaoh," Xander interjects, fiddling with the mysterious wooden box with the crescent-moon insignia on the table. "I mean, those pyramids, they practically build themselves."

Giles gives him an obligatory disapproving glance before continuing. "'What they discovered was that the pronounced suicide rate was caused by the arrival in their midst of a demon known as K'adolh, who dwelt along the riverbanks of the Nile, feeding off the misery of the enslaved. The Order of Shifrah managed to render K'adolh incorporeal, caging his essence within a papyrus leaf on which the binding spell is written.'" Your Watcher reaches over and takes the box from Xander. "This box bears the symbol of the order. It is in fact quite likely to contain the Shifran map, the tool they developed to track their nemesis."

"How did the Big, Bad, and Depressing manage to get out of this papyrus thingy?" you ask.

"'The demon,'" Giles continues, handing the box back to Xander and returning to the text, "'though physically powerless, escaped by entering the body of a human host, one of the pharaoh's guards who unwittingly seized the papyrus following a raid on the Order of Shifrah's makeshift temple. K'adolh then ripened the host from within by implanting dark thoughts in his mind and feeding off the resulting melancholia.

"'For sustenance K'adolh must move from person to person, jumping to the next host using paper as his conduit, leaving before his victim ends his or her own life. And so, it is said, K'adolh travels, continent to continent, throughout the ages, passing from hand to hand via the last piece of paper touched, be it a suicide note, a book, a bus ticket. As legend has it, K'adolh's best-known method of infection, a playing card, earned the king of hearts the nickname "the Suicide King." To this day the figure on this card is almost always depicted as a king putting a sword to his own head.'"

"If there's anything about a murderous old maid in there," Xander says, "I don't want to know."

"What's he looking for?" you ask. "What does he want?"

"I'm not entirely sure, but I suspect that his followers are planning something much greater." He places the open book on the table, the pages turned to a disturbing etching of a circle of demon worshippers clad in the skin of snakes. "The Cult of K'adolh, recognizable by sign of the *Naja haje,* or Egyptian cobra. The mortal enemies of the Order of Shifrah, the Cult of K'adolh seeks to recorporealize their demon king. If I had to venture a guess, I would posit that they are planning on using the confluence of mystical energies that is the Hellmouth to achieve their goal."

"Okay, so this K'adolh guy, right, he travels through the last piece of paper touched by his victims before they kill themselves," Xander says. "So, if we catch him between bodies, why can't we just, you know, burn whatever paper he's hiding in?"

"I don't know the answer to that," Giles replies. "None of the texts I've found have referred to that option. Perhaps destroying the paper actually sets him free. Otherwise, why would the order not destroy him when they first had the chance?"

"Maybe they were studying him," you speculate. "Maybe they thought there were more where he came from."

Xander takes up the box again, busily turning the mysterious wooden cube on its various sides. "How's it going?" you ask him.

"Nothing yet," he says, his frustration evident in his tone. "It doesn't seem to have a hinge or a catch of any kind. Not my kind of box."

"Keep trying," you say. "The sooner we figure out how to get the map out, the sooner we'll be able to find K'adolh." *Even if he's in this very room,* you think, harking back to this morning and the various papers belonging to the grief counselor you pored over in Snyder's office. *Please, God, don't let me be infected.*

"Hey, guys," Willow says, walking through the library's swinging doors.

"Hey, Will, what's shaking?" She looks like she's seen better days. Her skin is sallow, her eyes sunken; she instantly reminds you of what your mother looked like right before she and your dad separated. Seeing as how you've spent many an evening covered in blood and sweat and dirt, you decide not to draw attention to her appearance.

"Oh, no," Cordy says, throwing up a hand to block her view of Willow. "What happened to you? Didn't we just have a conversation about rouge not two weeks ago? I'm sorry, but you are offending me. You look awful. Even for you."

"I've just been having a really bad day," Willow says absently, sliding into a chair at the table. "Before you guys called, I was just going—"

"Whatever you're about to say," Cordy interrupts, "it better end in the words *extreme makeover.*"

"I was just going to meet a shrink my mother made an appointment with to talk about my blues." Silence. "Extreme makeover," she adds.

"Oh, God, I can't take this anymore!" Cordy screams, standing and pounding her fist against the tabletop with a loud *whack.* "It's bad enough that everybody in this town wants to kill themselves, but when this collective depression starts making people I have to hang out with look like—well, like *that,*" she says, gesturing at Willow before quickly averting her gaze once more, "then we have to find this thing before I'm cast out of society!" Cordelia pounds the table for effect again, only this time, with her head turned away, the heel of her fist comes down onto the wooden box. Instead of the expected wallop for emphasis, however, there is complete silence in the room, as her fist has not hit the surface of the box but entered into it, her hand obscured up to the wrist.

"Uh, guys," you say, "Cordy's figured out how to get into the box."

Giles pushes his glasses up onto the bridge of his nose and, with the rest of you, hurries over to her. "Of course," he says, marveling at the simplicity of it. "The key to the box is the pure and untainted desire to find the demon king."

"Hey, I wanted to find him too," Xander says, scowling. "Obviously I wasn't using the supreme and all-powerful force of Bitchcraft."

"Take a page," Cordy says, smirking, her hand still stuck inside the box.

"Cordelia," Giles says quietly, afraid to upset the balance of whatever mystical forces are at work, "I need you to concentrate very hard on your desire to find the suicide demon so that the map will be released."

Cordy rolls her eyes and says, "By the powers of Dolce and Gabbana, please let me help those less fashion forward than myself."

In an instant a ball of light explodes from the box, sending a violent wave of white electricity ripping through the room. Then it pulls back on itself, contracting. Everyone seems slightly dazed, though unaffected, until you see Xander back away from the table where Willow now sits alone, illuminated, her eyes glowing a shimmering, serpentine gold.

"So good of you to show yourself," Giles says with surprising calm, stepping between Willow and Cordy, whose eyes are wide with fear.

You watch your best friend's eyes slowly narrow, her lips curling up into a sinister smile. *"K'ADOLH,"* it says in a deep and booming cadence so very far from Willow's own voice. *"YOU MAY CALL ME K'ADOLH."*

SLAYER ACTION:
Turn to page 44.

"What do you think it is?" you ask Giles, who is sitting on his living-room couch, turning the wooden box with the crescent-moon insignia over on its various sides.

"I am entirely unsure. I can't seem to find a hinge or a catch of any kind. Besides, I'm not wholly convinced that opening this box without knowledge of its contents is necessarily the best plan of action." He sets the box down on the coffee table. "Tell me once more what you heard at the inn."

"It was kind of hard to understand what they were saying, seeing as how I was in the closet with the door shut," you say. "Something about the map being lost to the serpents—I think that's what's probably inside the box, a map of some kind. They knew exactly where to find it, at the bottom of the suitcase; they must have gotten that information from the grief counselor before he died. I also got the feeling that they were working with him somehow. They referred to someone as Tealius, which is awfully close to Teal, the counselor's last name, don't you think?"

"We can't be sure of that. Was there anything else?"

"They mentioned another person, Abraham or something, who they were hoping was keeping the box safe. I don't really remember anything else."

Giles gets up and goes over to his desk, retrieving several small volumes from one of the bottom drawers, and he begins quickly scanning the volumes' indexes, all the while muttering to himself under his breath. "Witchcraft . . . Tealius . . . Serpents . . . No, nothing here . . . Perhaps under the Artifacts Reference Table . . . Let's see, lunar symbology, maps . . . Aha!"

He pulls a larger text from his bookshelf, flipping to the middle of the book, and begins to read; a few moments later you notice the blood begin to drain from his face. "Good lord," he enunciates, lowering the book, his hands trembling. "Buffy, we're not safe here."

Suddenly all the lights in the apartment begin to flicker wildly. You watch the leather-bound volume slide out of your Watcher's hands, and when the book hits the floor, just before the electricity cuts out, you catch a startling image on its open pages of a scaly, snakelike demon with the words "K'adolh, the Suicide King" printed alongside the chilling etching.

You hear Giles cry out, and as you struggle to find him in the dark, you sense a strange paralysis beginning to take you over, causing your body to become heavy with pain, blocking off your air. You fall to the ground, clutching at your throat, and listen as Giles, between gasps, manages to utter, "Buffy, the box . . . destroy the box. . . ."

You try to crawl over to where the box rests on the coffee table, but every foot of ground gained feels like walking a mile in the most arid of deserts. You're still lucid, barely. You're just awake enough to hear the sound of footfall all around you. From where you lie on the floor, you can just make out the hooded figures surrounding you, their amber, snakelike eyes glowing like fireflies in the dark.

"We have come for the map," one of them says,

leaning toward you. You can see now that the golden eyes are merely decorative, sewn on to his robe's cowl; these are not the people you encountered at the bed-and-breakfast, but far more terrifying. "You and your pathetic order were fools to try and stop the Cunning One."

"Can't fault me for trying," you say, starting to fade from consciousness.

"All hail K'adolh," another intones.

"Hail K'adolh," the rest respond as one.

You want to fight, you really do, but you don't have an ounce of strength left in your body. Just before you black out, you see a pair of golden, serpentine eyes hovering above you, seemingly narrowing and coming closer, moving in for the kill.

THE END

"**I** would love to help you guys out," you whisper, "but I can't give you back this box if you're just going to use it to kill an innocent victim."

"May the Fates protect you, then," the white-clad man pronounces, "for we will not."

"Godspeed, Slayer," the woman says. Then, a single word: *"Sanveyr."* A moment later the two members of the Order of Shifrah vanish, leaving you alone in the dark room, the wooden box with the crescent-moon insignia still in your hands.

"Thanks a lot," you sigh, just before the door flies open. Three figures dressed in hooded robes storm into the room. On top of their sleek cowls are stitched narrow golden eyes, as if to replicate those of a snake, staring at you eerily out of the darkness. The lead Serpentine lunges at you, and you sidestep him, sending him crashing into the closet door with a backward kick. The other two begin to circle you, and you pivot, trying to keep against the wall, protecting your back. There's only so much you can do with the wooden box in your hands.

Suddenly, with a sharp hissing noise as your only warning, a warm liquid splashes over your neck. A moment later your esophagus begins to constrict, cutting off your supply of air. You stumble forward and fall to the floor, dropping the wooden box as you clutch at your throat, struggling for breath.

"The map!" one of your attackers yells before slamming against something in the dark. Still unable to breathe, you struggle to reach forward along the hard wood floor, trying desperately to reclaim the box. *It's not here,* you realize, your hands unable to find anything but empty space. There is a sharp cracking sound, and then another, as the last two standing members of the Cult of K'adolh are tidily dispatched, toppling like felled trees on either side of you.

Angel? you think, unable to speak, unable to breathe, as you begin to fade from consciousness.

"We are no angels," a woman's voice replies out loud to your private thought. The room begins to glow with a bright white light, and now you see her, crouching down beside you, the silver-haired woman with her fellow Order of Shifrah compatriot, who is cradling the wooden box in his hands. *They were here all along,* you begin to comprehend. *They were just invisible. . . .*

She places a hand on the back of your neck, and it feels cool and more pleasurable than any sensation you can remember. Suddenly you feel your throat begin to open, the burning pain dissolving away, replaced by a soothing, agreeable calm, the air rushing into your lungs once more.

"I'm very sorry," she says, restorative energies working through your body, healing you both physically and mentally. "We will use the map to find K'adolh this night and end his dark reign. It must happen our way."

"Okay," you say dreamily, drifting away. "Whatever you say."

SLAYER ACTION:
Turn to page 125.

You wake up in the morning in your own bed with such an unusual sense of ease and relaxation that you're immediately suspicious, but not sure why. You quickly dress and hurry downstairs, unclear about what happened the previous day; all you seem to remember is going to school and hearing that there was another suicide, and that the grief counselor was dead, and then, after that, the strange sensation of being bathed in a wonderful white light, enveloping you in warmth and comfort.

Joyce is sitting at the kitchen table with a cup of coffee, reading the local paper. "Hey, sleepyhead. Get a move on, or you're going to be late for school."

"Why didn't you wake me up?" you ask.

"You just looked so peaceful when I checked on you this morning, I didn't want to disturb you. What time did you go to bed? When I got home you were already asleep."

"Uh, I think around six or so," you say, but you have no real recollection. "I must have been really exhausted." Joyce stands up and abruptly sweeps you into her arms, hugging you almost to the point of suffocation. "This is nice, but . . . Mom, what's with the reverse Heimlich?"

"I'm just glad everything's fine, and I want you to be happy."

"All right, all right. Color me happy, okay?"

"It's just that I was reading in the paper about all the recent suicides and . . . I want you to come home right after school today. I'm worried for your generation, Buffy, I really am." She gets up and goes into the kitchen to replenish her cup of coffee, and you pick up the newspaper. On the cover is the story on the recent suicide epidemic, without mention, interestingly enough, of the grief counselor's death; as you read it, you begin to have a strange feeling that you've forgotten something important.

You turn the page and, in the bottom corner, see a story about three out-of-towners found dead the previous evening; the image of golden, snakelike eyes appears in your head, and your hand absently scratches at your throat before you turn the page again. On page five, however, a headline above a small item catches your attention—LOCAL BOY KILLED IN BIZARRE ACCIDENT—and you begin to read.

Thomas Morgan, 16, who was last seen alive walking home from practice for the Sunnydale Razorbacks junior varsity basketball squad, was apparently electrocuted, according to the coroner's office. His body was found early last evening on the docks, with the skin bleached to the bone from the accident and still emitting a strange white electrical current, making recovery of the body difficult for emergency medical technicians on the scene. Interestingly, a small but distinct mark in the shape of a half circle or moon was noticeable on the teen's forehead, and is considered a significant point of examination by forensic experts, as the catalyst for the fatal accident is still unknown.

You put the newspaper down and stare out the window. You remember now, everything: the demon contagion, his followers, and the Order of Shifrah, as well as the warm white light that surrounded you, healing you. And then you know. The order succeeded in destroying K'adolh, using the same energy used to revive you to kill the demon's current host, an innocent.

A heaviness weighs in the pit of your stomach, and you shudder; surely there was some other way.

THE END

"This is no mere childish diversion," Xander lectures, leaning over Giles's coffee table, intensity narrowing his eyes. "For if you choose to partake in this time-honored rite of passage, the stuff that legends are made of, in which the weak are unmasked for the cowards that they are, understand that the consequences are severe, and that we won't all make it back alive. This, ladies and gentlemen, is war." He turns over the first card in his half of the deck: a ten of spades. "Top that, little lady."

Willow slowly slides over her first card, playing it blindly. "Oh, look! A queen. I'll be taking that ten, thank you very much." She retrieves Xander's card, putting it at the bottom of her deck along with her own. You're all killing time, waiting for Anna and Ilon to muster enough energy to use the Shifran map. They're sitting cross-legged on the living-room floor, silently summoning their strength, Giles nervously perambulating back and forth while the rest of you play cards.

"Ah! My old friend, one-eyed jack." Xander nods, eagerly awaiting his prize, when Willow counters, turning over the king of hearts. "Ah, the Suicide King," he says ruefully, to which Anna makes a slight gesture with her hands, her index and middle finger, extended in the form of two fangs. "Not a fan, huh?" Xander says, to which she shakes her head.

"This card," Anna says, gesturing at the playing card, "with the king holding a knife to his head, is so depicted in honor of K'adolh the Nightwalker himself, who famously used to spread through playing cards as they traveled from hand to hand over the course of an evening's play. One man's good fortune meant another's doom."

"Maybe we should have gone with Yahtzee," Cordelia says, watching as Willow returns her half of the deck to the coffee table.

Suddenly all the lights in the apartment begin to flicker wildly before the power goes off entirely. As you struggle to orient yourself in the dark, you sense a strange paralysis beginning to take you over, causing your body to become heavy with pain, blocking off your air. Everyone around you seems affected as well, and you can hear the sound of bodies falling to the floor, one after the next. Finally you succumb as well, stumbling against the couch before dropping down to your knees.

You're still lucid, barely. You're just awake enough to sense footfall all around you. From where you kneel on the floor, you can make out the hooded figures surrounding you, the amber, snakelike eyes on their long cowls glowing like fireflies in the dark.

"You want that map so much?" you manage to get out between gasps. "Take it."

"We no longer have need for it," one of them says, leaning toward you. You can see now that the golden eyes are merely decorative, sewn on to his robe's cowl; these are not the people you encountered at the bed-and-breakfast, but far more terrifying. "We have already found our master's current vessel. We have come to destroy the remains of the Order of Shifrah. Tonight the Cunning One will be made whole, born into this world once more. All hail K'adolh."

"Hail K'adolh," the rest respond as one.

You want to fight, you really do, but you don't have an ounce of strength left in your body. You collapse and, just before you black out, you see a pair of golden, serpentine eyes hovering above you, seemingly narrowing and coming closer, moving in for the kill.

THE END

You pull a stake from your jacket pocket and take a deep breath before jumping out from behind the shipping crate and launching the sharpened projectile straight at Spike's back. In the instant between the stake leaving your hand and hitting its mark, Spike turns, plucking it from the air as if he has known you were there all along. "Oh, goody," he says, an expression of genuine excitement on his face. "I wasn't expecting you *this* soon."

"I aim to please," you reply, pulling another stake from your pocket as Drusilla scuttles back into the shadows of the factory floor.

"Your aim is in need of improvement." His arm extends, and you roll into a somersault as the stake you threw at him comes flying back at you, narrowly missing your head before embedding itself in a supporting beam with a sharp *thwack. Got to get him away from the hostage,* you think, returning to your feet, your fists at the ready. "It's been too long since I got to bag a slayer," he says, removing his black leather jacket while he slowly steps toward you. "If I'd known you were going to show up on your own, I would've asked that demon cult to bring me something new and shiny instead."

You look above you and see a retractable ladder stretching up to the walkway along the factory ceiling. Leaping up, you seize the bottom rung and slide it down along its track to the floor. "Where do you think you're going?" Spike snarls, his features transforming into his true vampiric face. He lunges at you from the other side of the ladder, throwing a punch through the rungs. You take it on the side of your head, and although it momentarily rattles your brain, it's worth the trouble when you reach forward and grab Spike by his bleach-blond hair, yanking the upper part of his torso through the ladder.

"Have a nice flight," you say, grabbing the sides of the ladder. You use all your strength to send the ladder back up its track, sending Spike, who's still stuck between the rungs, up with it. A brief second later, the ladder fully retracted, he hits the bottom of the iron catwalk high above the factory floor with a loud crunching noise. You quickly turn, hurrying over to the boy tied to the tabletop, and pull the piece of duct tape from his mouth. "You're going to be okay," you say, hurrying to undo the wire binding him. "I'll have you out of here in just one—"

"Get away from me!" he shrieks, his eyes frantic with fear. "If you untie me, it's going to kill me!"

"I'm not going to let anything happen to you. Everything's going to be—"

Suddenly a haunting voice begins to echo through the factory, singing a familiar tune. "La doo dum dee, ya dum dee doo. La doo dum me, ya dum dee you." You spin around, attempting to discern where Drusilla is, but her hypnotic voice is everywhere at once; after a few moments you find your hands letting go of the copper coils, dropping to your sides. You no longer remember what you're doing here, who you are.

She steps out of the shadows then, her face that of the undead, her pale form strangely mesmerizing; as she approaches you, you lock eyes. And that's when she has you. "Slayer," she singsongs, moving beneath the catwalk where Spike lies unconscious, still pinned by the ladder, "I have the most *beautiful* present for you."

"I love presents," you say blankly, your voice unfamiliar to you and coming from a faraway place.

The strange sound of your words momentarily snaps you back to reality and your terrible predicament, and you force yourself to concentrate and shake off the effects of Dru's mesmeric powers. There's a whisper of noise behind you. As an arm slips over your head, tightening around your neck, you realize that you're too late to react: Spike has regained consciousness and has you trapped in a headlock, his viselike grip slowly tightening, cutting off your air.

Drusilla walks over to where Spike holds you, standing just a foot away, her eyes aglow, enchanting. "A beautiful Angel gave it to me, and now I'm going to give it to you. Do you want the lovely present?" She runs her fingernail along the length of her forearm, and you watch in awe as a thin strand of blood trickles from her skin. You nod, utterly rapt.

In a few moments you will be dead. But by tomorrow evening you will rise again.

THE END

The psychiatric ward of Sunnydale General Hospital has its own waiting room, and its own particular ambience. Unlike the waiting rooms in the other wings, many of which you've frequented, this one does not have the strong smell of industrial cleansers to mask the unpleasant odors of human sickness. Rather, it has its own specific scent: the barely perceptible yet somehow still palpable stench of sadness. You crinkle your nose, slide back a bit on the plastic bench, and try to ignore it, but it just won't go away.

It's been three weeks since the night you performed the devocation ritual to exorcise K'adolh from the body of your best friend, trapping the demon forever in the hell dimension from whence he came. At first you were convinced you'd done the right thing, as you untied Willow from the chair and saw that she was still breathing normally. But then she looked up at you with that blank stare. . . .

"Miss Summers?" says the intake nurse, leaning forward across her desk, and you quickly stand. "You can see her now. Last room on the right at the end of the hall."

You open the door and your heart breaks. Willow is sitting in a wheelchair by the window, facing into the room with the sunlight at her back; she has the same affectless expression she had immediately following the exorcism. It's the first time she's been allowed visitors, and you were hoping for some, any, improvement in her condition.

"Hey, Will," you say quietly, slowly closing the door behind you. "How's it going?" She doesn't reply, which is no surprise, as she hasn't spoken a word to anyone. You would do anything to hear her voice again.

You pull a chair up beside her and reach into your bag, pulling out a stuffed animal you bought at the hospital gift shop. "I got you this. I hope you like it." You place the fuzzy blue cat in her hands, and she seems to grasp it for a moment before letting it fall to the floor. You reach down and pick it up, returning it to her lap.

If only I could take it back, you think, fighting back the tears. *If only it could have happened differently.*

It's then that you decide that you won't stop until you find some way to heal her, no matter what the cost. Dark magicks, black market deals, whatever it takes. You know that if the situation were reversed, Willow would find a way to help you.

You take her hand in yours and squeeze it tightly. *I'm going to make it right, Willow. I'm going to bring you back.*

You move her wheelchair so that she's facing the window, the sunlight streaming across her face, and it almost looks as if she's smiling.

THE END

If you don't hand over the scroll, K'adolh is going to use his power to force the hostage to cut his own throat. In all the time you've been the Slayer, never have you been faced with such a difficult decision, and you refuse to have his blood on your hands. You don't really see another way out.

With a heaviness in your heart, you assent to the demon's wishes. The nearest Serpentine quickly steps forward, retrieving the scroll from your outstretched hand.

"You have chosen wisely, Slayer," K'adolh hisses through the mouth of the boy as he lowers the knife from his neck. *"My body made flesh once more is but an inevitability. You will be in a position of honor as you bear witness to my rise."*

The Serpentines march you and your friends over to the far wall of the factory, where they begin to tie you all to a grated divider with strong copper wire. "Buffy," Giles begins to say as he's bound alongside you, "how could you . . ." and then stops; he knows the difficulty of your decision. You're forced to watch as the dark practitioners position their candles, incense, and a ceremonial sword needed for the recorporealization spell.

"We call forth K'adolh, King of Despair," the hooded worshippers chant in a circle surrounding the hostage. *"Come forward, and step into this mortal plane."* One of them blows out his candle, and the demon hisses through the boy's lips as it is slowly wrenched out of him.

"We beseech thee, Demon Lord, walk amongst us once more, and take your rightful place on the throne of all creation." Another candle is extinguished, and the air begins to crackle with golden electricity.

"Leave your prison of flesh, and join your subjects in the waking world." Smoke begins to rise from the boy's flesh; a long, gurgling scream escapes his lips.

"Your time is now, your time is always. . . . Lead us into the darkening hour." The boy is quieted as a glowing wraithlike form floats into the air above him. It's not fully formed but flickering, here one moment and gone the next, a translucent humanoid shape stretched out from head to foot, a long mane of hair whipping back and forth like a snake struggling to free itself from a predator's grasp.

"Dark K'adolh, King K'adolh, we bring you forth. Dark K'adolh, King K'adolh," they continue, the air positively alive with unholy energy. *"Show us yourself in all your infinite glory."*

With that, the Cult of K'adolh extinguishes the last remaining candle, and, save one final burst of light and fire, the factory is pitched into total darkness. Suddenly there are screams, everywhere at once, and you can hear the horrifying sound of the Suicide King as he devours his followers one by one. Just above the din you can make out the sound of heavy footsteps as K'adolh makes his way across the factory floor; you struggle to break free of the copper bindings, using all your strength, but to no avail.

As you smell the stale breath of despair descend over you, you think of the next Slayer who will rise in your place, and pray that she shows no mercy.

THE END

You're certainly not going to hand over the scroll to the demon's dark practitioners, but even if you don't destroy the scroll, how can you hope to stop K'adolh from killing his hostage? You have to act now, and you don't really see another way out. You look to Giles, who gives you the slightest of nods, before you proceed to rip apart the ancient scroll.

"No!" one of the Serpentines screams before they descend upon you, swarming, trying to get at pieces of the scroll as they spill from your hands, flittering from between your fingers like ash from a toppled censer. Giles spins, batting away a cultist before punching the hostage in the face, knocking him to the ground. The loud sound of the knife hitting the factory floor causes a Serpentine to turn from you, tackling Giles instead. It seems that everyone is in the fray, Xander and Cordy battling back your hooded assailants with grim determination, while Willow leaves Anna's side and yanks some loose copper wire from the tabletop, bringing it over the head of one of the Serpentines and using it as an effective garrote, wrestling him to the ground.

We're winning! you exclaim to yourself in glee, just before you feel the unexpected sensation of a warm liquid splash over your neck. You turn to see a cultist holding some sort of blowgun in the shape of a coiled snake; a moment later your esophagus begins to constrict, cutting off your supply of air. You stumble forward and fall to the floor as you clutch at your throat, struggling for breath. The factory melee begins to fade into the background as you crawl under the table for protection, your strength draining from you.

Suddenly a large bright light appears, and you wonder if you're starting to hallucinate. But then you see: It's Anna, crouching over you, her silver hair falling in her face, the blood from her wound a dark stain on her otherwise pristine white robes. "Slayer," she speaks inside your mind, "thanks to your sacrifice, we shall attain victory."

Yeah, well, you're welcome, you think, and she smiles in response to your private thought before pulling up the sleeves of her robe. Anna places a hand on the back of your neck; it feels cool and more pleasurable than any sensation you can remember. Suddenly you feel your throat begin to open, the burning pain dissolving away, replaced by a soothing, agreeable calm, the air rushing into your lungs once more.

"I'm very sorry," she says, out loud now, restorative energies working through your body, healing you both physically and mentally. "The Serpentines have poisoned you with their venom. But soon your pain will be but a memory. Or perhaps, not even that."

"You're hurt yourself," you manage to get out, drifting rapidly from consciousness in a haze of whiteness.

"What, this?" she says, gesturing to her stomach with her free hand. "This is nothing in the face of our mission. We will achieve success this hour. But it must happen our way."

"Okay," you say dreamily, the world falling away. "Whatever you say."

SLAYER ACTION:
Turn to page 125.

You knock repeatedly on the front door of the Collins house, and a young boy, about ten or so, finally answers, opening it just a crack. "Hi," you say with a little wave. "Are you Madison's little brother?"

"Uh, yeah," he replies hesitantly. "One of them. Jeff."

"Hi, Jeff, my name's Buffy. I . . . went to school with Madison."

"Oh. Hi." *He looks a little scared,* you think. "Is there something I can help you with?"

"Do you mind if I come in and talk to you?"

"Well, there's no one else home."

"Don't worry. I won't bite."

You watch him look up in the sky, noting that the sun has yet to set, before he looks back at you. "Yeah, okay," he says, nodding. "But my parents are gonna be home soon."

"It'll only take a minute." He swings the door open and lets you walk inside, then he looks out onto the street and shuts the door closed behind you. "I wanted to ask you about your brother's accident. I'm . . . doing some research on all the recent suicides at our school, and—"

"My brother didn't kill himself; he had an allergic reaction. That's how he died."

"Listen, Jeff," you bluff, "I looked up Madison's medical records in the nurse's office, and he didn't have any allergies. I don't think that's what happened, and if you know anything, I could really use your help. There are lives at stake."

He looks at the floor, nervously hops from one foot to another, and then sighs. "I may know something."

He gestures for you to follow him upstairs and leads you into Madison's room, which is perfectly ordinary in its usual teenage disarray; you wouldn't be surprised if it hadn't been touched since the day he died. "Over there," Jeff says, pointing to his brother's desk.

You walk over and see, on top of a typical wreckage of papers, video game cartridges, and tattoo magazines, a deck of playing cards, the king of hearts on top. You're not exactly sure what he's trying to show you, so you reach down for the playing cards; when you do, Jeff jumps forward to stop you. "Don't touch them!" he screams, pulling your arm back. "He told me never to touch them."

"What? These cards?"

"Yeah. He said they were talking to him. He said they told him to kill himself."

"He said what? Are you sure?"

"He said a lot of things since he came home with those cards. Most of it didn't make any sense. The voices, they were in his head, telling him bad things. But it started with the cards."

"Let me ask you, did Madison know a girl named Barbara O'Hearn, by any chance?" At the mention of the name, the boy's face turns white, and he almost looks like he's going to pass out. "What is it, Jeff?"

"Barbie . . . she was my math tutor. She killed herself too."

"Were she and your brother friends?"

"No. That's the weird thing. They didn't know each other at all."

"Did they have any contact that you can think of?"

"No, nothing. I was always talking about how they should meet, but they never did." He pauses for a moment, then says, "There was one thing . . ."

"You can tell me," you say, leaning down a bit to look him in the eye. "I just want to make it stop."

"He bought a pair of tickets to go to a jazz festival, before he . . ." Jeff swallows hard before continuing. "My mom, she found the tickets in an envelope in his pants pocket and gave them to Barbie as thanks for being such a big help with my math. She really liked jazz and stuff like that."

Playing cards? Concert tickets? Suicide notes? What's going on here? "Was there anything else he said, anything at all that could help me figure out what's going on?"

"Not really . . . Just to stay away from the abandoned factory on Highland Street. He caught me playing outside there a few days before he died and told me vampires lived in there." *Not that factory,* you think, the hair on the back of your neck bristling.

"You know what?" you say. "Your brother was a smart guy. And you must take after him, the way you checked to see if the sun was still up before inviting me in."

"You saw me do that?" he says, his eyes widening in awe.

"I notice these things." You tussle his hair; you've always secretly wanted a little brother or sister. "Thanks, Jeff. You've been a big help."

As you step outside the Collins house, you notice that the sun is now beginning its slow descent into night, and you raise the collar on your leather jacket. Maybe it's a coincidence that Madison told his little brother to stay away from that factory; however, that's a risk you can't afford to take. You weren't planning on having to tangle with them over this suicide business, but if that's what's in the cards . . .

"La doo dum dee, ya dum dee doo. La doo dum me, ya dum dee you."

You creep along the walkway bordering the factory, watching Drusilla warily from above; she doesn't seem to sense your presence. She's too busy singing to herself, dancing about the room with a Victorian doll in her hands. At least she seems distracted; she's brittle and somewhat sickly, but you're still unsure of the depths of her legendary powers. You make your way down to the factory floor, crouching behind a shipping crate just before the door bursts open.

"You've brought the kitten!" Dru howls, clapping her hands.

"I told you I would, didn't I?" Spike boasts, storming into the room with his typical swagger, dragging something heavy in his wake. You can't see what's going on, and you're not entirely sure you want to. "Now we wait for the Demon Aid Society to bring us our finder's fee, and lo and behold, all our dreams come true."

"Miss Edith doesn't like dreaming," Dru says, a shudder in her voice. "It makes her hungry for bones."

"Well, give a doll a bone, then," Spike says, tossing

something on the table in front of him. "Give me a minute, love. Got some trussing to do."

You can hear the sound of tape being ripped, and after a minute or so you lift your head up ever so slightly to peer over the crate. Tied to the tabletop in what appear to be thick coils of copper wire is an extremely tall boy about your age, a piece of duct tape covering his mouth. He is completely motionless, save his eyes, which are darting back and forth, wild with fear. You've seen enough.

SLAYER ACTION:
Turn to page 131.

The stairway quickly fills with smoke and, as you make your way down, you are finding it increasingly difficult to support Willow's weight and hold on to the wooden box at the same time. "Here, hold this," you say, handing her the box as you take her under the shoulder. Suddenly a white ball of pure energy explodes from the surface of the box, knocking both of you off your feet and sending you careening down the staircase. Once you hit the landing, your shoulder wrenching, you turn, dazed. Willow is still halfway up the flight of stairs and completely immobilized. You hurry back up but, just as you're about to reach her, two of the hooded cultists round the corner, the serpentine eyes of their cowls shining in the light of the fire. They trap you, standing on either side of Willow's frighteningly still body.

You do the only thing you can think of and grab Willow before they can, shielding her as much as possible before you smash through the banister, dropping to the floor ten feet below. Before you can regain your footing and lift her in your arms once again, you feel a warm liquid spatter the back of your head and neck. You turn and see one of the goons holding some sort of blowgun in the shape of a coiled snake; a moment later, your esophagus begins to constrict, cutting off your supply of air. You stumble forward and fall to the floor as you clutch at your throat, struggling for breath.

"Willow . . ." You gasp and try your best to remain lucid. In a few moments, however, you hear the unwelcome sound of footsteps.

"Foolish girl," one of your assailants sneers, his

fellow dark practitioners busily hoisting Willow on their backs. "You have lost this war. K'adolh the Nightwalker will rise once more, and for the last time, as it is prophesied."

As they carry her down the stairs, away, all you can think of is her, even as you slowly begin to lose consciousness, the building burning all around you.

THE END

Sheila Rosenberg, Willow's mom, answers the door, opening it just a crack.

"Hey, Mrs. Rosenberg. Can I talk to Willow?"

"I'm sorry, Bunny, but she's really not feeling well. We think she should just stay in with us tonight."

"Oh, I don't need her to come out. It'll only take a minute."

"That's not going to be possible. She'll see you in school tomorrow." And with that, she shuts the door, end of discussion. *Okay,* you think, *that went well. . . .*

You step off the porch and start down the street. You need to get some information, and fast. It's possible Giles is aware of some kind of demonic power or magickal rite that could be responsible for these suicides. Knowing him, he's probably still lurking in the library, shelving books or doing the research thing. If he's never heard of a paranormal cause for suicide, hopefully he'll be able to find it in one of his many volumes of material on the occult. *Back to school we go. . . .*

Just then you see some rustling in the row of hedges behind Willow's backyard. It's still a little too light out to be a vamp, but it could be any number of other things, from an evil cat to a stray demon; couldn't hurt to check. You look both ways to make sure no one's around before making a beeline through the yard of the neighboring house, slipping behind some trees and into the shadows. You crouch down, tiptoeing your way through the underbrush, stopping behind a low hedge to take a peek at what may be lurking.

Directly behind the Rosenberg property you see

three men in dark brown robes with long hoods pulled down over their faces. Atop their sleek cowls are stitched narrow golden eyes, as if to replicate those of a snake, the image of which causes you to shiver. They're huddled around something, and you crane your neck to get a closer look. In one of their hands is a wooden box inscribed with a crescent-moon insignia. What's most alarming about the box, however, is an intense white glow emanating from somewhere inside. The light appears to be pulsating, but doing so in such a swift manner that the shine is almost steadily intense, like a rapid-fire strobe.

"He's close," one of them says in a low whisper. "The hour is at hand."

"Hey, guys," you say, stepping out from behind the bushes. "I was just looking for my old Lite-Brite and— oh, I see you found it." Before they can react, you deliver a roundhouse kick to the head of the one holding the box, knocking him to the ground. Another of the goons grabs your arm, but you're too fast, flipping him over your back before punching him in the chest. The one holding the box drops it, and the moment it leaves his hands it ceases glowing before hitting the hard earth.

Your eyes go to the box and its crescent-moon insignia, silver inlaid. You reach down to grab it, but just before you do, you feel the unexpected sensation of a warm liquid splashing the back of your neck. You turn to see the remaining hooded figure holding some sort of blowgun in the shape of a coiled snake; a moment later your esophagus begins to constrict, cutting off your supply of air. You stumble forward and fall to the floor as you clutch at your throat, struggling for breath.

"The map is ours now, Shifran," he says, standing over you, still clutching the blowgun in his hand. "You cannot stop the rise of the Cunning One."

"Well, I gave it my best shot," you struggle to say, rapidly fading from consciousness.

You watch him as he reaches down and picks up the box, the pulsating light returning to its frantic pace as he grabs it. As he leans over you, the last things you see are those golden, serpentine eyes, seemingly narrowing as everything fades to black.

THE END

ABOUT THE AUTHOR

Robert Joseph Levy is an author of numerous stories and plays whose work has been seen off Broadway. He studied writing at Oberlin before graduating from Harvard and earning a Master of Arts degree in forensic psychology at John Jay College of Criminal Justice (CUNY). His first contribution to the Buffyverse, "Back to the Garden," appears in *Tales of the Slayer, Volume 4*. Robert's online home, where his latest work can be found, is www.robertjosephlevy.com. He lives in Brooklyn, New York.